Adam P
Eerie Deirdi

Illustrated by Teri Smyth

FOR...
Mum — the Queen on her throne.
Dad — the Troll under her bridge.
My Joanne — The Princess to this Frog Prince, the Beauty to this Beast.
And, of course, for my Caleb — The little Goblin who has us all under his spell...

ACKNOWLEGEMENTS...
My heartiest of heartfelt thanks must go to :
Dawn — for elongating my hyphens and rampant red-pennery. I've learned so much, thank you.
Teri — for squiggles and scrawls and keeping your composure whilst dealing with an imagination like mine (more piratey, more captainy — the latter not actually being a word recognised in any of the known tongues of men).
And to Vicky — for even more rampant red-pennery than Dawn, for taking a gamble and for turning this writer into an author.
The cliché that if I were to list all the people I wanted to, it would take a novel in itself is unfortunately very true. So thank you to all my family and all those wondrous friends that have been so genuinely excited and have been counting down the days with me (I know who you are, even if you don't). It will not be forgotten. Ever.

A catalogue record for this book is available from the British Library
ISBN 978-0955903915

Printed and bound in the UK by Direct-POD www.direct-pod.com
for Clementine Publishing
Walsh Fold, Bolton
Book design by Teri Smyth

Visit us at www.clementinepublishing.com
and www.eeriedeirdredarkly.com

Publishing

CONTENTS

PROLOGUE

(Which means the beginning bit, you know, before the actual story.)

When an escaped lunatic comes up to you in the street wearing a green and yellow striped bathing costume, singing about woodlice and strumming on a broken banjo he has named Dennis, the best thing to do is run away.

Fast.

As fast as you can, in fact.

Faster than a Taiwanese Zippy Fish in August (when they are at their fastest).

But when this very thing happened to my great-great-great-great-great uncle, he didn't run. He stayed still.

Very still.

Stiller than a Taiwanese Zippy Fish in April (when they are at their stillest).

If the escaped lunatic wearing the green and yellow striped bathing costume, singing about woodlice and strumming on a broken banjo named Dennis gives you a hand-drawn map of a strange county you have never heard of, then you should forget all about the Taiwanese Zippy Fish, fall down where you are and pretend to be dead until he goes away.

But not my great-great-great-great-great uncle. Oh no. He took the map and used it as his favourite napkin until the day he died. After he died he found he didn't have much use for it so it was passed down to his son, who used it as a handkerchief. The son after that used it to stop a table wobbling so he could stand on it to change a light bulb. The son after that used the map to give paper cuts in the street to passing fishmongers (he hated fish and all who monged them). Until, eventually it was passed down to me. After scraping the map clean of all the sausage fat and bean juice, bright-green nose gravy, table-leg rust and the blood of countless angry fishmongers, I followed it.

I ventured forth to the strange county of Glumshire with nothing but my wits, a compass and a cross-eyed pack mule named Pedro. In hindsight, I should have taken a coat as well. It was freezing. And taking a pack mule (cross-eyed or not) just to carry my compass was a bit excessive.

Pedro and I soon discovered that Glumshire was an extremely large county filled with villages. Lots of villages and each one stranger than the last. But by far the two strangest villages of all were Gravely Down and Grimley-by-the-Sea…

These two villages are geographically quite close to one another and both are very isolated from any other village in Glumshire. So you would be forgiven for thinking that the inhabitants would be incredibly neighbourly, indeed the best of friends.
You would be wrong!

The villagers of Gravely Down have long since regarded their neighbours with a deep suspicion bordering on fear. The villages are only separated by a long, thin, winding mountain path. It climbs from Gravely Down up to Grimley, which sits on a cliff-top overlooking a stormy sea. But as far as any Gravely Downian is concerned, 'Them up on the hill' can never be far enough away. You see, for centuries it has been the custom of the Gravely residents to complain about their neighbours. Constantly.

"There's strange noises at night-time! Howls and growls and rumbles!"

"It's constantly raining!" another might add. "It's not natural!"

"There are weird flashes of lightning!"

"They never come down here!"

"They're just plain STRANGE!" they all cry in unison.

This is where our stripy-suited escaped lunatic comes in. One Wednesday morning in the year 1789, Arthur Witt, local explorer and village madman, decided to put an end to all the rumours. Taking with him some sandwiches, a notebook, a pair of Wellington boots and a broken banjo he had named Dennis, he made his way boldly up the mountain path. Arthur was gone for several weeks and the residents of Gravely Down soon tired of waiting for him to return. They all assumed he was dead. Or indulging in his favourite pastime of sitting in a tin bath full of mango-flavoured jelly singing, There's a Naughty Little Goblin Who Lives in My Sock, at the top of his voice. There's a Naughty Little Goblin Who Lives in My Sock was a song of his own composition which he played on Dennis the broken banjo at any and every available opportunity. It would, eventually, become the village anthem of Gravely Down.

Imagine their surprise then when one dull morning Arthur Witt came skipping down the path whistling the song I Like Woodlice, They Are My Friends. Incidentally, this was his second most famous composition and was the B-side to There's a Naughty Little Goblin Who Lives in My Sock. He was taken at once to the nearest pub (The Angry Melon) so everyone could hear his tales of 'Them up on the hill'. Every man, woman, child and chicken in the village piled in after him and gathered round as Arthur drank deeply and told them all exactly what he had seen.

"Them..." he whispered. Everyone (and the chickens) leaned in closer. "Them up on the hill..."

"Yes...?" said a boorish baker.

"Them up on the hill..."

"Go on...!" said an impatient poultry farmer.

"Them folk up that there hill..."

"GET ON WITH IT!" shouted an irate author.

"Them up on that hill... are all... monsters!" Every man, woman, child and chicken in the village looked at one another.

Monsters?

What did he mean?

"He's mad!" said the boorish baker.

"A babbling buffoon!" cried the impatient poultry farmer.

"Sing There's a Naughty Little Goblin Who Lives in My Sock!" bellowed the irate author.

Arthur confirmed calmly and rationally that the residents of Grimley-by-the-Sea were indeed all monsters. Vampires, werewolves, mummies and zombies and so on. He went on to say that he was greeted most politely by them and that they even gave him a guided tour of their village. Apparently, the village itself was more or less exactly like Gravely Down; though it was, mysteriously, much larger than it appeared from the bottom of the hill. The monsters above, he declared, were simply trying to get on with things away from the prying eyes of the rest of the world.

Well, this did not sit well with the villagers of Gravely Down for two reasons.

1 They didn't really like the idea that there were (man-eating?) monsters living in the next village.

And 2. This revelation might severely damage their chances of winning the coveted Glumshire in Gloom Award for the twenty-eighth time in a row. And so they did what all slug-brained morons do when faced with a problem of such monstrous magnitude.

They ignored it.

Every man, woman, child and chicken left The Angry Melon muttering and shaking their heads. And beaks. But mostly their heads.

"Well I never," said the impatient poultry farmer, "that's the last time I put my faith in a man with a fondness for broken banjos and baths full of mango-flavoured jelly."

"Aye," said the boorish baker, "if only there'd been some sign he was mad."

"And," the irate author piped in, "he never sung There's a Naughty Little Goblin Who Lives in My Sock!"

Poor old Arthur Witt was taken to Miss Sickle's Home for the Gibberingly Insane and locked away in a tiny cell with only a bucket, a toothpick and a mouse called Alan for company. He wasn't heard of again for many years, until one Tuesday afternoon when he escaped. He managed to trick a flock of passing seagulls into thinking he was a very large mackerel and they swooped down and carried him away to safety. Once free, he hadn't much time to give my great-great-great-great-great uncle the map he had made using only a toothpick and half a yellow crayon Alan had managed to smuggle in. He was soon discovered by Miss Sickle herself (she had simply followed the trail of seagull droppings), who dragged him back to the asylum kicking and screaming. Poor old Arthur wasn't too happy about it either.

When he was once more safely inside his tiny cell, the villagers of Gravely Down pushed him out of their tiny minds and tried to go about their business as usual. They tried very hard to forget Arthur's insistence that there were monsters living happily in the village above them. Though all of a sudden a lot of things made much more sense.

Now that they thought about it, the strange howling noises they had always blamed on the wind did actually sound a bit, well, wolfish. The rumbles they had always thought were falling rocks may well have been, as Arthur had said, giants playing football in the mountains with huge boulders. It was also extremely strange that Grimley-by-the-Sea should get so many lightning storms and so much rain when Gravely Down did not. Could it be as Arthur had said? Was the lightning really created by crazed scientists in their laboratories? Was the rain merely a side-effect of the magic in the air from the dozens of witches and wizards? And as for why none of them had ever visited, well, if they were monsters they most likely would keep themselves to themselves…

Soon enough the Mayor of Gravely Down, Mr Ezekiel Prong, declared that no-one from Gravely Down was ever to set foot anywhere near Grimley-by-the-Sea. EVER. Well, ever again. The law was passed and every man, woman, child and chicken in Gravely Down became even more fearful of the village above them. The only time 'That Village' was ever mentioned was by parents of children who would not do as they were told.

"If you don't eat your parsnips," they would say, "I'll send you up th' hill!" Needless to say, the parsnips did not stay on the children's plates for long.

Of course we all know that monsters don't exist.

Well.

Actually.

Yes, they do.

Old Arthur Witt was right. About everything. The cliff-top village of Grimley-by-the-Sea is completely inhabited by monsters. Old monsters, young monsters, monsters you would recognise in an instant, others that would make you stop and scratch your head. Friendly monsters, scary monsters and some monsters that are so frightening they would make your eyes cross, your head spin and your hair turn into cabbage leaves.

Despite this, most of the inhabitants of Grimley-by-the-Sea are honest, hardworking folk who have lived there for years. Mr Stokes the butcher, for example, is quite the jolliest vampire you'll ever meet, if not a bit scruffy and slightly overweight. It isn't entirely his fault though. After all, he can't see his reflection.

Mr Tut, on the other hand, was banished from

his home in Egypt after he was woken up by some clumsy archaeologist named Lord Rodney Costingstock III. Lord Rodney claimed he was looking for Tut anyway, but then panicked at the sight of him and was last seen running down a sand dune screaming, "MUMMY!" Mr Tut found himself in a situation thousands of monsters before him have faced since the dawn of time; chased from their homes, banished from their towns and cities and left with nowhere else to go. But a monster in need will always be greeted with open arms in Grimley-by-the-Sea.

Or with open tentacles.

Or claws.

Or pincers.

Or — well, you get the idea.

Not that, I should point out, they like to be called 'monsters'. They much prefer the term Fright Folk, which was coined centuries ago by monsters who disliked being referred to as monstrous. Back then they all agreed that, to some, they may well appear frightening (and villagers armed with pitchforks and flaming torches were certainly evidence of this) but there is more to a being, monster or otherwise, than what you see on the outside. And so the term "Fright Folk" was born.

Despite knowing that humans find them scary, the Fright Folk don't sneak off at night to go 'scaring' or 'haunting' in the village below.

Although they could…

And some of the younger ones do…

But they shouldn't!

However, there is no actual law in Grimley that

forbids any resident going to visit their neighbours if their intentions are not mischievous or frightening. Most of them, however, choose not to go at all. Some can't see the point in visiting the village that has won Glumshire in Gloom twenty-seven times in a row. Others have lived with humans most of their lives and are, quite frankly, sick of the sight of us. But most of them are afraid. That's right, monsters that are afraid of humans! It's not unheard of. Actually it's quite common. Even professional wrestling superstar Mad Martha McMangle the Masked Minotaur and her Menagerie of Menacing Minions are too afraid to go down there.

So, how extraordinary then to find our story beginning with a 10-year-old resident of Grimley-by-the-Sea making her way to Gravely Down? In particular to Gravely Down Junior School. But then again, she is an extraordinary little girl...

Mrs Cowl is a withered old vulture of a woman with a wrinkled face that seems to have a permanent sneer stapled upon it.

CHAPTER 1
DEIRDRE DARKLY

Deirdre Darkly is ten years old and of average height for her age. She has rather pale skin and black hair which she normally wears in two bunches. A relatively well-behaved girl, she doesn't give her parents or teachers too many reasons to shout at her. So, in many ways, she is a very normal girl indeed. However, in other ways, she is very, very different.

For example, Deirdre Darkly likes spiders. All spiders, of every shape and size. She even has a pet tarantula called Treacle who can normally be found napping in her school satchel. Deirdre also likes other 'creepy' creatures, like bats and earwigs, and isn't afraid of the dark either. She likes nothing better than curling up in bed at night with a scary book and a mug of steaming hot chocolate, Treacle snoring gently away on her bedside table.

But what makes her even more different is the fact that she is a monster. I don't mean that she's horrible — she doesn't go around poking badgers with sticks or flicking mud at kittens or anything — I mean she is a real life monster: wings, tail, the lot. As with most monsters, Deirdre has Camouflage, which means she can disguise herself as a Typical whenever she needs to. A Typical (for those of you who don't know) is what monsters call people who aren't monsters. To them we are just so ordinary and there are so many of us that we are just plain Typical. So every morning, Deirdre dons her Camouflage — which is about as comfortable for a monster as you or I walking around in soaking wet clothes all day — and sets off for school.

An old, horse-drawn carriage rattles her noisily down the pass that spirals from Grimley-by-the-Sea to her school in Gravely Down. So as not to arouse too much suspicion from her schoolmates, the carriage stops behind a large boulder at the bottom of the pass and she walks the rest of the way.

You may think it odd that there is a large boulder conveniently placed at the end of this path. In truth, the boulder is a lasting monument to one of the last great sporting spectacles in the history of Grimley-by-the-Sea — The Skull-Crusher Cup Match of 1893. You see, every seven years since 1705, a game of football was played high up in the mountains between two warring giant families — the McCraggs and the Grumbols. For ninety minutes every seven years, eleven members from each family would put aside their differences and play a nice, friendly game of football. Well, they played a game of football. Alright, a game of blood-filled, bone-breaking, teeth-shattering, eye-gouging, no rules, no holds-barred football. It was quickly recognised (by those brave enough to watch) that the game was merely an excuse for the families to beat the bogies out of each other. Needless to say, by the end referees for the match were getting extremely hard to find. The Skull-Crusher Cup has not been held for many years now, not least because the death count had reached epic proportions. (In fact, so many referee lives hadn't been lost since the Forty-Ninth Annual Referee Convention of 1773 was gate crashed by a short-sighted polar bear who mistook them for very tall penguins. The organisers agreed that holding it at the North Pole was a mistake and promised that if it was ever held there again then they would invite plenty of vicars and nuns to give the referees a sporting chance.) But the main reason for the Cup's cancellation is that during the Cup Match of 1893, an over-excited striker, named Bonehead McGragg, booted the boulder they were using as a ball so hard it flew right out of the stadium. It even flew right out of Grimley and landed with a sickening splat on a group of birdwatchers from Gravely Down. Their joy at having just spied a Lesser-spotted Yellow and Green Worm-Warbler was rather short-lived. As, in fact, were they. Needless to say, the bird flew off and the Gravely Down Twitching Association did not meet together much after that. It was soon decided that, if such occurrences continued, The Skull-Crusher Cup could possibly start drawing unwanted attention to Grimley-by-the-Sea and therefore it was abandoned. Thankfully, most of the Gravely Downians thought the rock had fallen because of an avalanche in the mountains above. Those who had guessed the real cause for the demise of the Gravely Down Twitching Association kept their mouths shut and simply hummed I'm the Queen of Lollipops (another of Arthur Witt's Greatest Hits — watch out for the album release some time in June) until they forgot what they were worried about. The villagers of Gravely call it the Offside Boulder because of the way it leans precariously to one side. Strangely enough, the residents of Grimley call it by exactly the same name. It is still an ongoing debate amongst sporting enthusiasts whether or not Bonehead McCragg was offside or not when he kicked it. Despite its bloody history, Deirdre Darkly is very appreciative of Bonehead McCragg for putting it there as it gives her a perfect hiding place from which to start her walk to school.

Deirdre rather enjoys the walk through Gravely Down. It is usually the best part of the day. When she was first sent to a Typical school, it had been quite exciting. Her parents thought that it would be good for her to experience Typical life for a few years before she started secondary school in Grimley. However, nearly two years on and the excitement is well and truly wearing off. It doesn't help that while she is stuck studying pointless subjects like Maths and Food Technology, her friends back in Grimley are studying subjects such as Mad Science and Frightology.

And as if that isn't bad enough, for a non-monster school, she has managed to end up with the most monstrous teacher of all. Mrs Cowl. Mrs Cowl is a withered old vulture of a woman, with a wrinkled face that seems to have a permanent sneer stapled upon it. She seems to delight in picking on Deirdre at every available opportunity. Even when she doesn't have her hand up in Maths, Mrs Cowl always picks on her to answer questions. And once, when Alice Brigstock was copying from Deirdre's paper in a spelling test, it was Deirdre who got in trouble for talking when she told her to stop! Deirdre didn't know how she had done it, but Mrs Cowl had managed to stay as her teacher for two years instead of one. The children of Gravely Down Junior School all secretly believed that Mrs Cowl had kidnapped Mr Pratt (the previous Year 6 teacher) and had locked him in the class store-room. It made sense, as none of the children were ever allowed in there. Deirdre thought it more likely, however, that Mrs Cowl just wanted to see her suffer for an extra year.

It's a difficult job being a monster in a Typical

school. Deirdre has to be careful what she says and how she behaves, so as not to reveal her true identity. She can't have any friends over to her house for tea (not literally for tea — she's not that kind of monster!) or a sleepover because the place is full of monsters. And the food... Deirdre can't really stand Typical food. But what monster of taste would enjoy gravy made from meat instead of slugs' blood? Or baked beans instead of frogspawn? Or fishfingers instead of maggots in mouldy batter?

The only thing that makes school almost bearable is Jenny Froggett. Jenny is probably Deirdre's best friend in Gravely Down Junior School. She has been ever since Deirdre joined Mrs Cowl's class in Year 4. Mrs Cowl had charged Jenny with the job of 'looking after the new girl' in that awkward way teachers will when a new pupil arrives. Most of Deirdre's classmates started avoiding her in the corridors and the playground when one of them had spotted Deirdre getting out of the old rickety carriage near the Offside Boulder. Their parents had obviously told them horror stories of the strange goings-on and the odd folk that lived in Grimley-by-the-Sea and this, combined with Deirdre's old-fashioned clothes and love of creepy-crawlies, made her something of an oddity. But apart from a few funny looks in her first year at Gravely Down, it didn't really bother her that much. Everyone nowadays treats her more or less pleasantly enough.

Except for a girl named Millicent Parpington.

Millicent Parpington is a girl in Deirdre's class. Her father is Dr Theodore Parpington, a very rich and very famous doctor, and Millicent loves nothing more than bragging about how much money they have.

"Oh," she said loudly as Deirdre entered the schoolyard that morning, "Daddy says he's going to buy me another pony because Sugarlump is sick and if he sneezes too hard I might fall off and hurt myself."

"Or the poor horse might throw you off because he's sick of you," Deirdre muttered to Jenny as they waited for the bell to ring. Jenny snorted loudly and Millicent spun around on the spot. Seeing Deirdre and Jenny her angry red face suddenly turned into a happy red face.

"Oh look," she shouted even louder, "it's Eerie Deirdre! What on earth are you wearing Eerie Deirdre? I think my Grandma has the same dress!" Millicent pointed a sausage-like finger at Deirdre's red dress. True, it was rather faded and certainly very old (it actually had once belonged to her grandmother) but it was one of her favourites. She loved wearing the old-fashioned hand-me-downs her Mother and Grandmother found for her in the old travelling chests and the huge carved wardrobes at home. They made Deirdre stand out from everyone else, which was always a good thing.

Millicent's large gang of friends began to snigger at Deirdre and some of them started muttering to each other and pointing. Deirdre felt her face flush angrily, but not at the comment Millicent had made about her clothes. Millicent had started the nickname 'Eerie Deirdre' two years ago when Deirdre had started at the school. Unfortunately, it had stuck and now everybody seemed to use it.

"Maybe you'd like my old horse," Millicent

continued through her fake giggles, "it might scare off some of the bats in your attic!"

Deirdre scowled at Millicent. She liked the bats in her attic. They were nice bats. And what was wrong with having bats in your attic? But before she could say anything in return, Mrs Cowl entered the playground, her long black dress swishing behind her. Her claw-like fingers clutched the school bell, ringing it to signal the start of the day. At once, Millicent Parpington turned and ran off to where Mrs Cowl stood, standing before her like an obedient puppy. Deirdre thought that if Millicent had a tail it would definitely be wagging.

"You should've set Treacle on her," said Jenny, glaring at the back of Millicent's stupid head. It really was a stupid head, full of flouncing curls and a huge pink headband with a large butterfly on it.

"Nah," said Deirdre, "it wouldn't be fair on Treacle."

As the rest of the school filed in, Deirdre and Jenny hung up their coats and went into their classroom. It was a dull room, with nothing much in the way of decoration except a blackboard and several cobwebs in the corners of the ceiling. Mrs Cowl began her lesson as she did every day.

"Get out your Maths books," she droned. "We shall be continuing our work on long division."

Deirdre groaned. Not long division. Anything but long division. Well, except more Maths. Anything but Maths was generally her rule for a good day. Millicent Parpington was sitting four desks in front of her and right in front of Mrs Cowl. Millicent

Parpington. Perfect Parpington with her bags of cash and her pocketful of ponies. Millicent Parpington with her bags of cash, pocketful of ponies and her stupid head full of stupid flouncing curls. Almost as if she had heard Deirdre's thoughts, Millicent's hand shot into the air and she stood up as if hoisted on an invisible fishing line.

"Please Mrs Cowl!"

Mrs Cowl looked over her half-moon glasses and smiled at Millicent. This made Deirdre angrier than ever. If anyone else had interrupted they would have been in detention until they were twenty.
"What is it, Millicent dear?"

"Please Mrs Cowl, my daddy says that I can have another pony because Sugarlump is sick and he might throw me off him if he's sick, Mrs Cowl!"

"How lovely Millicent dear," simpered Mrs Cowl, "what a lucky girl you are." She turned to the blackboard and began writing long division problems. Deirdre felt her face flush with anger once more. Lucky girl?! Spoiled brat more like. All of a sudden she felt her head tingling, her eyes burning and a churning feeling in her stomach. She took a deep, soothing breath and tried to calm herself down. She recognised these feelings at once and knew that if she didn't control herself then something bad was going to happen. Something VERY bad indeed.

Millicent plonked herself back down in her chair. Deirdre glared at the back of her (stupid) head. She felt the tingling once more and reminded herself of what would happen if she let herself lose control. Breathing deeper still she was just beginning to feel her racing heartbeat slow down when Millicent's hand shot up into the air once again, dragging the rest of her with it. However, in an over-eager attempt to keep Mrs Cowl's attention she accidentally knocked her chair too far backwards. It was no longer underneath her bottom.

"Please Mrs Cowl!"

Mrs Cowl turned and looked at her again, smiling, as if there was no bigger joy in the world than two interruptions from Millicent Parpington.

"Yes, Millicent dear?"

Millicent ran her hands down her sickening floral yellow dress, flattening imaginary creases. "Please Mrs Cowl, do you like my new dress? Daddy had it shipped over from America, Mrs Cowl. Isn't it lovely?"

"Very nice, Millicent dear," said Mrs Cowl with another simpering smile.

"Thank you Mrs Cowl," Millicent replied, sounding surprised as if Mrs Cowl had complimented her dress without being prompted. "I think it's so important to look nice for school and not come dressed in old Granny clothes..." She shot Deirdre the briefest of sly glances before turning back to Mrs Cowl.

"Quite right too, dear," said Mrs Cowl turning back to the blackboard.

The smile on Millicent Parpington's face as she turned back around to look at Deirdre made the fading sensations inside her increase a thousand fold. She suddenly felt as though there were red hot spots inside her skin, bursting to get out. Millicent went to sit back down on her chair. A chair, she was to discover far too late, that was no longer where it should have been. She

25

fell, gave a startled yelp like a frightened poodle, and landed on her bottom with a loud smack accompanied by a ripping sound as her precious American dress caught on her upturned chair. The noise (loud as it was) made the entire class turn and look at her, almost all of them already stifling giggles. Mrs Cowl spun around and glared about the room, her wicked little eyes darting back and forth searching for a culprit.

Someone sniggered.

Someone else chuckled.

A short guffaw was heard and then...

Riotous laughter broke out from the entire class. Even Millicent's friends found it hard to control their cacklings. Millicent Parpington burst into floods of tears.

Mrs Cowl was the only one who didn't find it funny and she tried (very unsuccessfully) to quieten the class down several times. Deirdre tried her best not to laugh too much but, in the end, she succumbed to guffawing heartily along with the rest of the class. Looking around at the sea of laughing faces she happened to glance down at her hands, the sight of which stopped her laughing at once. It was, in fact, all she could do to stop herself screaming. Her hands had grown longer and more crooked, somewhat like a bird's. Her fingernails had grown into what looked like black, hooked claws. She quickly hid them under the desk before anyone could see, accidentally scratching a long, deep groove in her desk top in the process. She was trembling all over now.

"Not here..." she whispered frantically to

herself. "Not now…!"

She slowly and discreetly brought her hands back out from under her desk, half closing her eyes for fear of what she might see. But they were back to normal. Thank goodness for that, she thought. The long, deep-cut groove across her desk, however, would be much harder to hide…

CHAPTER 2
MEET THE DARKLYS

Until the bell rang for hometime, Deirdre could not get the 'incident' with Millicent Parpington out of her head. Nor could she stop looking at her hands every four seconds or so for fear of them transforming again. They had never transformed so completely before. Blackened, sharper fingernails, yes, or the tough, leathery skin perhaps, but never entirely.

Mrs Cowl had spent the rest of the day looking very accusingly at the class in that way teachers do — as if the guilty party might suddenly throw themselves down on the ground and beg for forgiveness. She sent Millicent home with a very bruised bottom to go with her newly ripped dress and gave the rest of the class a very long and extremely boring lecture on the dangers of pranks and practical jokes. Unfortunately, the class had all been too busy sniggering to themselves and remembering the startled look on Millicent's rosy-cheeked face to take any notice.

The hometime bell sounded the end of an otherwise normal day. Before she went home, Deirdre quickly swapped her freshly scratched desk with Millicent Parpington's. It was a rare act of naughtiness, but if anyone deserved it Millicent Parpington did. Deirdre then ran out of the school gates as fast as she could and made straight for the Offside Boulder.

Deirdre was picked up and dropped off everyday by a tall, thin and very scruffy man named Mr Prendergast. What his first name was Deirdre did not know. She had never asked and he had never told her. Now she thought about it, the only time she could actually remember hearing Mr Prendergast speak was the time he had mistaken a live rattlesnake for his belt and tied it round his waist. Although it has to be said that shrieking like an angry howler monkey and cursing this and all rattlesnakes until the end of time does not necessarily count as a conversation. He was an odd fellow, who always wore the same tatty brown suit jacket and a crooked top hat with a yellowing patch, sewn on crookedly. Fingerless grey woollen gloves and a battered old pipe that trailed constantly from his thin-lipped mouth completed the look. Twice a day he drove a small and extremely rickety carriage pulled by a small and even more rickety horse all the way up and down the pass between the villages.

Deirdre would normally spend the long journeys to and from school with her head in a book, or else hurriedly scribbling down her homework at the last minute. From her bag she took out her copy of The Adventures of Arabella Drabble by Seamus Digweed and began to read. The Arabella Drabble books were one of Deirdre's favourite series and this latest adventure — Arabella Drabble and the Typical Tyrant — was perhaps the best one yet. They were all about a monster detective and her talking cat, Claude, who worked undercover in the Typical world solving crimes that no Typical detective could solve. Arabella was one of Deirdre's favourite literary characters. When she had first started school in Gravely Down, she would pretend that she too was an undercover monster detective keeping an eye on suspicious Typicals. She read half a page of The Typical Tyrant but found that her heart wasn't in it. She couldn't get the day's events out of her head. She spent the rest of the journey looking out of the window as the carriage climbed higher and higher toward Grimley-by-the-Sea, leaving Gravely Down far behind.

Darkly Manor, Deirdre's home, stands at the end of a winding gravel drive and is perched on a small rise overlooking the whole of Grimley-by-the-Sea. Apart from the vast mountain range known locally as the Perilous Peaks, it is the first building you see on rounding the last bend of the mountain path. It is a dark, murky sort of house and almost everything from the front doorknocker (a grubby silver toad) to the weather vane (a great black bat) is crooked. It looks almost as if an angry giant had one day lifted the whole house from its foundations and simply dropped it back down again. Which may well have been the case. It is an exceedingly large house, far too spacious for the number of people who live there. So, the Darkly family had long ago decided to turn it into a grand hotel, the first and only hotel in Grimley-by-the-Sea. As such, it is normally terribly busy with Fright Folk coming from all over the world visiting friends and relatives, or else just taking a break from the stresses and strains of constant hiding and persecution. A large number of the guests are older monsters who are thinking of retiring here and want to visit the place first.

Inside Darkly Manor it is almost constantly gloomy. Flickering candles and large lanterns provide the light, as well as huge iron candelabras that hang from the ceiling on chains. The first room you see upon entering is (oddly enough) the entrance hall, which is a large room dotted with several chairs and a threadbare red and gold carpet. At the far end of the entrance hall is the reception desk, where the guests confirm their room reservations or make any special requests for their rooms (more damp and mud for swamp-dwelling guests, or blacked-out windows for those allergic to daylight). Scratching posts and chew toys are often required for guests of a feral nature, werewolves and suchlike.

As Deirdre stepped inside, a tiny gremlin called Willy Sprinkles was standing on the reception desk demanding a stepladder so that he might use the toilet without getting his new hat wet. Mrs Orrell the ogress was also at reception asking for a vegetarian meal at dinnertime as she said she was trying to vary her diet. At the moment it consisted of raw flesh, raw flesh and then a bit more raw flesh. So far during her stay she had eaten raw flesh, raw flesh, then a bit more raw flesh and half a garden salad. It was a start.

"Good evenin' Deirdre," came a voice as Deirdre wiped her feet on the doormat.

Deirdre looked up, "Hello Wilhelmina," she said distractedly. Wilhelmina was the Head Housekeeper and Nanny to Deirdre's baby brother Errol. She was a short, plump lady with rosy cheeks and a fierce temper when crossed. This didn't happen too often as whenever she was in charge, she ran the Darkly Manor Hotel like a captain runs a ship. Wilhelmina seemed to have the ability to carry out around forty-nine different tasks at once without even breaking into a sweat. She was also the clumsiest woman in Grimley-by-the-Sea and perhaps the entire world. While it was true that she held the house record for 'Most Plates Broken in Under a Minute' and 'Most Times Falling Down the

Stairs in The Same Day', the Darkly family would not be able to function without her. Even now she was somehow managing to give Errol his bottle with one hand, whilst carrying a colossal basket of washing in the other. This perhaps wouldn't be so hard if she hadn't also been trying to make her way down into the wash-room in the basement by opening the door with her feet. Maybe even this wouldn't be so hard if there weren't also several large sputtering candles in a silver candle holder balanced on top of the pile of washing.

"You look a million miles away Deirdre, are you alright?"

"Fine thanks," said Deirdre, eyeing the potential catastrophe before her. "Just a long day at school."

"Well you won't be there much longer will you deary-ducks?" Wilhelmina had successfully managed to push the door open with her foot. "Term's almost over and soon you'll turn eleven and it's off to secondary school you go." Wilhelmina turned on the spot to smile at Deirdre, but, instead of smiling lost her footing, flung a giggling Errol high into the air and fell spectacularly backwards down the rickety wooden stairs. She landed with a deafening crash at the bottom. Deirdre caught Errol with ease (she had had plenty of practice) and gave her brother a kiss; in return he gave her a toothy grin.

"Dinner'll be ready about six!" Wilhelmina called brightly from the bottom of the stairs. She then began whistling merrily as if a quick tumble backwards down a wooden flight of stairs was quite a part of her everyday duties. Which, now Deirdre thought about it, it usually was. As she shifted Errol to her hip, a loud snort drew her attention to the wall in front of her. Overlooking reception and framed on a large wooden shield was Barry the stuffed zombie moose head. He was, as usual, snoring gently.

Barry had been a fixture in Darkly Manor since the very first Darklys had lived there. In fact, it was Duke Cuthbert Fortescue Darkly, the first Earl of Darkly (and full time Typical) who had shot him, had him stuffed and framed him on his shield. Barry had his revenge though. The next night he had come back to life again as Cuthbert Fortescue was sitting down to his evening cup of tea. The old man had just realised that he had forgotten his customary four and a half sugars and so had reached behind to grasp the sugar tongs. It was then that he saw Barry with the sugar tongs clamped in his mouth, grinning and mumbling, "One lump or two?" Duke Cuthbert Fortescue Darkly was, quite literally, scared to death.

Standing beneath Barry behind the reception desk were Mr and Mrs Darkly. They were both scribbling things down busily in the hotel guest log as several more guests entered the lobby in anticipation of dinner.

Mr Dexter Darkly, Deirdre's father, was the head of the household and joint manager of the Darkly Manor Hotel. He was a tall, kind-faced man with neat brown hair, glasses and a liking for stripy tank-tops and large bowties. Darcy Darkly, Deirdre's mother, was a pretty, tall and graceful lady who was just as pleasant as her husband but not one to be crossed. Deirdre hardly noticed that her parents were Camouflaged, it wasn't an unusual sight when they were very busy.

33

Sometimes in stressful circumstances Fright Folk can Camouflage themselves or drop their Camouflage without even realising it. This can be quite problematic for monsters attempting to live and work in the Typical world. Just ask Mr Worming the demon primary school teacher, who once got so annoyed at his class he accidentally breathed fire at them. Two things were never the same again after that day. His class never misbehaved and their eyebrows never grew back.

"Mr Lestadt in room 203 has asked for more mouthwash," said Mrs Darkly to Mr Darkly. "He says there was a hint of garlic in his Bolognese. I know for a fact there wasn't, but you know what they're like."

"I certainly do," said Mr Darkly sympathetically, "someone should have a word with Auguste..." he hesitated as if about to ask his wife something.

Mrs Darkly sighed, put down her pen and said, "Would you like me to do it?"

Mr Darkly sighed gratefully, "Would you dear? I'd appreciate it awfully. You know how he gets about his cooking. Remember that time a guest complained about his goulash and he bit them on the shin?"

"Vividly," Mrs Darkly replied. "I'll tell him after tea tonight. And I'll put on shin-pads just in case. Don't forget that he wants to try out some new recipes on us all later, before he unveils them to the guests. And you wouldn't like to find any garlic in your food for offending him, would you?"

"Oh yes, I'd quite forgotten about that," Mr Darkly replied, smacking his lips. "And no I wouldn't!" He was just realising how hungry he was and how much he utterly detested garlic when he caught sight of Deirdre walking toward him with Errol in her arms. "Oh, hello Deirdre, good day at school?"

"Not bad," said Deirdre going behind the reception desk and handing Errol to her mother. "Hi Mum."

"Hello Deirdre," said Mrs Darkly, taking Errol and giving him a kiss. "Would you be a dear and take this tray up to Mr Lees in room 314? He says his dog is still very thirsty." Mrs Darkly gestured to a colossal silver tray on which were three huge bowls of water. "Oh and this," she reached behind the reception desk once more and pulled out a colossal slab of meat, raw and dripping blood. "It's Kevin's feeding time. Thank you, dear." She slapped the slab of raw meat on to a separate tray and handed it to Deirdre. "And don't forget to dress for dinner tonight," she added, "Auguste is trying out some new recipes and you know how he likes his diners to make an effort."

At that moment there was a grunt, a snore and a wheezing cough from above. The three Darklys looked as one to the stuffed moose head, which was now yawning widely showing huge, yellow teeth connected by gooey strands of saliva. "Did someone say dinner?"

"Ah! Good afternoon, Barry," said Mr Darkly smiling. "Pleasant nap?"

"Not bad, not bad," said Barry, half yawning and half chomping in anticipation of dinner, "I don't suppose there's any food going now, is there?"

"You'll have to wait until dinner, Barry," said Mrs Darkly, also smiling.

"Shame," said Barry licking his lips.

"I'll save you something," said Deirdre.

"Thank you." Barry looked as though he was falling asleep again.

"Don't let Auguste know his finest cuisine is being used to feed…" Mr Darkly gestured with his head up at Barry who, fortunately, had already fallen back to sleep.

"We won't dear," said Mrs Darkly. "Now Deirdre, room 314 if you please and don't forget Kevin."

Sighing, Deirdre put the smaller tray on the larger tray and struggled over to the lift, where an ever-sullen-faced gigantic ape stood waiting with the lift doors open. He wore a rather shabby, ill-fitting and tattered red tailcoat and a patched red bellboy's hat.

"Going up…?" he said in a voice so low it rattled Deirdre's bones.

"Room 314 please, Graham," said Deirdre, struggling to keep the three bowls from sloshing their contents all over the lift and herself. The lift cage clanged shut and began to rise, slowly at first but gaining speed, all the way up to room 314. When at last it came to a halt she struggled out and along the dimly lit corridor. Setting the tray down she knocked on the door and was instantly greeted by the sound of ferocious barking from within.

She heard a strong, low voice bellow, "Down, Cerberus, down I say!" followed by a whimpering and then silence. "Who is it?" came the voice again.

"It's the water you asked for? For your dog?" Deirdre's voice sounded weak and tiny after the huge dog's bark and the booming man's voice.

"Thank you," came the voice once more, "I'd

leave it there if I were you. He tends to get a little nervous around strangers."

Deirdre didn't need to be told twice. She grabbed the tray with the steak on it, turned from the door and almost ran down the corridor toward the staircase. She took the stairs three at a time, careful not to let the raw steak splash blood anywhere on the carpet or on her dress. She was on the very top floor of the hotel now. She jumped for the length of cord attached to the trapdoor above, grabbed it between two fingers and pulled down the fold-away ladder that led up to the attic. As soon as the trapdoor opened, there was a scurry of movement inside. Probably rats, Deirdre thought, but then reminded herself that Kevin had long since eaten all the rats in the huge attic. She climbed the stairs quietly and lit the candle that awaited her at the attic entrance. With the candle holder in one hand and the steak in the other, she crept as quietly as she could into the dark. It was a small candle and only lit a small area in front of her. She reached the middle of the attic and looked around, but there was no sign of Kevin anywhere. He must be out hunting, Deirdre thought, and placed the plate in the middle of the floor before turning to leave.

At that moment there came a terrific whooshing sound from above her, followed by a tremendous gust of wind. Deirdre felt something heavy barge into her, knocking her to the ground. She turned on to her back and saw the huge, beaked face of Kevin the pterodactyl staring back down at her. His row of tiny, razor-sharp teeth glinted in the candlelight.

"Get off, you overgrown budgie," Deirdre

giggled as Kevin gave her a friendly lick. "Get off!" Kevin wriggled and twisted his head for Deirdre to scratch behind his ears. He gambolled around the attic for a few seconds before devouring the dripping steak from the plate in one gulp. He squawked at Deirdre, who went over to the window and opened it. Kevin half-flapped, half-ran over to the open window before turning to Deirdre expectantly.

"I can't tonight, Kevin," she said, patting him on the head apologetically, "I've got to have dinner with my family downstairs." Kevin whimpered and hung his huge head sadly. "I promise we'll race tomorrow night though." He perked up a bit at this, gave her a final farewell lick and then disappeared out of the window and into the darkening night. Deirdre blew out her candle before heading back downstairs.

CHAPTER 3
UNCLE DILBERT

As she made her way through the hotel, Deirdre had the familiar feeling of safety she got whenever she came home. She would forget, when she left for school each day, just how much she missed the place when she wasn't there. The huge and immaculate kitchens of Darkly Manor easily outshone the filthy, stain-riddled and strange-smelling kitchens of Gravely Down. When she was stuck in her cold classroom or the pathetic school library (which contained just three books — two of them The Gravely Down Guide to Owls and the third The Gravely Down Owl-Spotter's Guidebook), Deirdre would think longingly of the cosy lounge and of all the books waiting for her at home.

Nowhere was as much fun as Darkly Manor. The constant gloom and the shadows cast by flickering candles made games of hide-and-seek a lot more entertaining than playing in a school playground. When younger cousins or friends of the family came to visit, they would spend hours creeping around the place, avoiding guests and hiding in shadowy corners. However, it wasn't so much fun on the rare occasions she could convince Treacle or her Dad to play. They were both hopeless at hide-and-seek. Treacle would usually give up after five minutes and sneak off to the kitchens, only to be chased out seconds later by Monsieur Volcan — the Head Chef — snapping at his heels. Or snapping at whatever the tarantula equivalent of heels are. The only time that Mr Darkly had ever won a game was the time he had hidden in an old suit of armour on the fifth floor and had become stuck. The only guest on the fifth floor at the time was Unbalanced Clarence the Pockmarked Poltergeist (who spent all his time shouting at mangoes), so Mr Darkly's cries for help went unheard. When he was eventually discovered (nine and a half hours later) he was fast asleep and snoring through the visor. Jokes about Mr Darkly 'getting a good knight's sleep' were compulsory at Darkly Manor for months afterwards.

Another of Deirdre's favourite pastimes was sitting in the great glass conservatory that overlooked the vast and untidy gardens. Sometimes, she and Grandpa Horace would sit there with a cup of tea while he told her tall tales about life in Grimley when he was a young pup. Sometimes she would simply sit there with her nose in a good book, occasionally looking up to observe the wildlife attacking the plant life, or vice versa.

But of all the other rooms at Darkly Manor, it was the great library with its rolling ladder and its thousands and thousands of books that she loved the most. For hours she would lose herself in tales of adventure and discovery in far-off lands. Fright-Folk explorers were all so much more interesting than the Typical explorers she read about at the school in Gravely Down. She was often amazed by how many Typical explorers took credit for a monster explorer's accomplishments. For example, the first female ever to fly solo across the Atlantic Ocean wasn't the Typical pilot Amelia Earhart. Every monster knew it was the gargoyle adventurer Lady Felicity Pennyfeather who accomplished it in just under an hour thanks to a good tailwind. Another example was Captain P. Stirling's ill-fated return journey from the South Pole in 1912.

During the expedition, Major Fitzwilliam Bakewell bravely sacrificed himself for the good of his fellow explorers. He walked out into a raging blizzard muttering the words — "I'm just nipping out for a packet of crisps and some blue tack..." Every Typical thinks he froze to death. Fright-Folk history books, however, give a different account. Major Bakewell secretly went outside to participate in the 23rd Annual Charity South Pole Swing-Ball Tournament. This is a yearly event between the yetis and the abominable snowmen with all proceeds going to the very worthy cause 'Plimsolls for Penguins'. The rest of the expedition froze their nose-hairs off, while he warmed up quite nicely with a few rounds of swing-ball. Major Bakewell liked the company of yetis so much he decided to stay, and was last seen working at Brisk Bob's Discount Sleigh Station — where he eventually worked his way up to Assistant Manager. Deirdre knew this version was true. When she was seven, she had actually heard the story first-hand from a very old yeti named Cyril who had once stayed at Darkly Manor.

Meeting the foreign monsters that would often pass through was one of the best things about living in a hotel. There were so many exotic visitors from strange and far-off places, who brought with them weird and wonderful stories that Deirdre could listen to for hours. She had always thought she would like to see the world one day. Perhaps she could be a famous explorer charting the uncharted for all of monster-kind. Or she could even discover lost treasures and hidden artefacts and bring them back home to be placed in the Grimley Museum of Unnatural History. Her daydreams often saw her being rewarded for her exploits with a great, gleaming medal presented to her by the Mayor of Grimley-by-the-Sea himself, Hugo Ghastly.

Lost in her thoughts, Deirdre reached the east wing of the hotel, where all the family lived together. Her bedroom was at the very highest level of the house up a narrow, winding staircase. It was almost perfectly round and it was Deirdre's second favourite room (after the library) in the entire house. Sitting heavily on her bed she threw her school satchel down beside her and said, "Wake up, it'll be tea-time soon."

Something moved inside the bag. A small, slow-moving lump made its way to the open flap and out stepped a rather groggy and grumpy-looking tarantula.

"What time is it?" Treacle yawned, blinking several eyes as they grew accustomed to the light.

"Almost half five," said Deirdre looking at her watch. "Had an exciting day?"

"Oh," said Treacle, stifling another yawn, "you know how it is."

"I do," said Deirdre, with a half-smile, "sleep, sleep and… oh yes, more sleep. Then break-time: eat, eat and eat some more. After that it's time for some serious sleeping until lunchtime when… let me see… you eat again. And then—"

"Alright, alright," said Treacle, "you do go on. Have you got my glasses?"

Deirdre reached inside her dress pocket and pulled out a small box that had once contained Mr Mollusc's Mighty Mint Mites — the minty mite with the peppermint bite and opened it. She carefully removed

42

a pair of tiny spectacles with eight lenses, and placed them over Treacle's many eyes.

"You know," she began as Treacle blinked several eyes several times, "there's not much point coming to school with me if all you're going to do is sleep and eat in my bag all day. You could do that at home. Not to mention the mess you make of my books."

"We've been over this a thousand times," Treacle replied lazily. "I accompany you to school to keep several eyes on you. We can't have you transforming into your natural state in front of all your little school friends and causing a panic. You're at a delicate age, Deirdre, and it's difficult to keep your Camouflage on for long periods of time."

"Well, you weren't much help this morning," Deirdre muttered irritably.

"I can't very well go out on patrol, can I? I'm not as young as I was, plus I'll cause a panic if I'm seen — Wait a minute — what did you say?"

Deirdre sighed, "I nearly dropped my Camouflage in class this morning."

"What?" Treacle was wide awake now. "Did anyone see? How bad was it?"

"Nobody saw," said Deirdre. "I knew you'd overreact. It was just my hands and I hid them as soon as I saw them."

"Oh this is no good, no good at all," Treacle began to pace back and forth. "You should never have gone to that school, I said it from the start!"

"Mum and Dad wanted to give me a taste of the Typical world."

"You should have stayed at Grimley Primary,

I've always thought so!"

"Alright," said Deirdre smirking, "no need to start climbing the walls…"

"This isn't funny, Deirdre," said Treacle.

"I'm not laughing!"

"You're smirking!"

"I didn't say I wasn't smirking. There aren't any No Smirking signs in my room."

"Deirdre this is serious," snapped Treacle. "You don't need me to tell you what would happen if…" he shuddered. "Well you won't be at that school much longer, that's some comfort I suppose."

"Look, just don't tell Mum and Dad, alright?"

Treacle stopped his pacing and looked at her. "I don't know, Deirdre. I'm supposed to report back on anything of note and this — a partial transformation — is definitely noteworthy."

"It was nothing," said Deirdre, almost trying to convince herself as well as trying to forget how scared she had been, "just leave it, okay? No-one got hurt. Except a desk. And it was an old desk, it didn't have any family or anything."

"Deirdre…"

"Alright! Sorry. Like you said, I'll be out of there soon anyway. And good riddance!"

"I don't know…"

"Come on…" Deirdre pleaded. "Just leave it, will you?

"Deirdre, I'm sorry," said Treacle pompously, starting to pace again, "but I am honour bound to report any and all—"

"Look," said Deirdre getting an idea, "it's a

special dinner tonight. Why don't you go and sneak a peek in the kitchens and see what we're having while I get dressed up?"

Treacle stopped his pacing. This mention of food had done exactly what Deirdre had hoped it would. It made Treacle forget all about telling her off. He was clearly torn between the two for a good three seconds or so, but soon scuttled out of the room as fast as his eight legs could carry him.

Pleased with her ingenuity, Deirdre found a smart, black evening dress and changed into it. After a quick glance in the mirror she left her room thinking she would spend the last few minutes before dinner in the library.

As she rounded a corner, however, she almost ran headfirst into a short, chubby man wearing stained blue overalls and a red and gold bandana. His face was round and even grimier than his clothes, and he had a long, thick, black moustache that covered his top lip entirely and hung down almost to his double chin. He had a toolbox in one hand, a large wrench in the other and a half-eaten corned beef sandwich sticking out of his mouth.

"Alright Deedee?" he said, smiling through a mouth full of soggy corned beef, margarine and bread. "How was school?"

"Hello Uncle Dilbert," said Deirdre, smiling and wondering why everyone she knew asked her the same question the minute she got home. How good could one day in school be? "It was the same as always."

Uncle Dilbert pulled a face, "That bad, eh? Wanna help me fix a toilet before tea?"

From anyone else this would seem a very unappealing proposal. But when it was from Uncle Dilbert you knew you were in for more fun than fixing a toilet usually warranted. Uncle Dilbert was Mrs Darkly's brother and the hotel handyman. The main problem with this arrangement was that he couldn't really fix anything. He tried his best, but his best usually ended up either exploding in a ball of flames or else never working in quite the same way again. For example, the time he had tried to fix the toaster, it had somehow come to life and started spitting red-hot pieces of burnt toast at people while it ran around the kitchen growling. Then there was the time he 'fixed' the lift. For two weeks afterwards, instead of merely going up and down, it went from side to side. To this day no-one is really quite sure how. When he finally got it moving in the right direction again, instead of sending people to their rooms, it started sending them through time and space. Poor Mrs Batley, an elderly vampire, was just trying to get to her room one night and instead ended up in ancient Rome in an arena full of man-eating lions. Luckily, she had her umbrella with her and managed to fend them off before leaping back inside and closing the grille.

Deirdre and Uncle Dilbert made their way to the third-floor toilets, checked to see if they were empty, then went inside.

"This is the one," said Uncle Dilbert, gesturing with his wrench to the fifth cubicle along. It was oozing with a strange, green slime and was bubbling over like a boiling cauldron. The floor of the cubicle was already full of the stuff but it was so thick and slow-moving it hadn't yet spread to the rest of the bathroom. Uncle Dilbert knelt down in the foul sludge as if it was sweet spring water that he was about to bathe in and shoved his gloved hands into the toilet bowl.

"Eww, what is that?" asked Deirdre.

"There's a family of spectres in Room 304, got twin boys about your age. Bet they've been dive-bombin' in here, leaving ectoplasm all over the place... Pass us that plunger, will you?" he gestured with his head toward his toolbox. Deirdre passed him a long red plunger with which he began to attack the toilet with gusto. "So," he said over the loud squelching noise, "anything interesting happen today?"

Deirdre sighed quietly. What was it with her family and school? She supposed it was because she went to a 'normal' school that everyone was concerned in that annoying, repetitive way that families enjoy so much. "Fine," she said, non-committally. Then, before she could stop herself she added, "I nearly lost control of my Camouflage this morning."

Uncle Dilbert stopped his rampant plunging and turned to look at her, his mouth slightly open. Deirdre didn't quite know why she had told her uncle about her accidental slip earlier that day. She was incredibly fond of him. He made her laugh and was more fun than most grown-ups she knew, but she never normally confided in him. If anyone, it was Treacle she would tell this sort of thing to, and no-one else.

"You what?" Uncle Dilbert pulled off his rubber gloves and threw them back in his toolbox, the ever-growing foul, green sludge momentarily forgotten.

"It was nothing," Deirdre backtracked, "no-one saw."

"Good thing too," said Uncle Dilbert, doing his best to sound
authoritative and almost managing it. "How often does this happen?"

"Never!" said Deirdre indignantly, "I can't even remember the last time." She normally had a good degree of control over her Camouflage and resented the accusation that she was constantly slipping into her natural state all over the place. "I was just angry, that's all."

"Well," said Uncle Dilbert huffily, "you'll be leaving soon at any rate. I always said it was a mistake sending you there. Too dangerous, I said, but no-one ever listens to me."

"What did you say?" Deirdre smirked.

"Very funny," Uncle Dilbert's moustache twitched slightly as he tried to hide a smile. He adjusted the tool belt that was almost hidden by his huge belly and sniffed loudly. "Never had that problem myself. Camouflage I mean. Not like your Mum, we wizards mostly look just like Typicals."

Deirdre looked her Uncle Dilbert up and down. Of all the family members she could think of, she thought he would be the one who might value Camouflage the most. It would have been cheeky (even for her) to say this, so she contented herself with watching in silence as he continued to plunge away. After a few more minutes he put his plunger down and wiped the sweat from his brow, getting green goo all across his forehead in the process.

"This is no good," he sighed, reaching for his toolbox and pulling out a small wooden box with chewed metal bars at one end. From the scurrying, scratching noises there was obviously something alive inside it. "When all else fails..." Uncle Dilbert gave Deirdre a wink before sliding the box open. Out plopped a huge, purple snail with a lime-green shell, two huge antennae and a tremendous set of sharp teeth.

"What's that?" Deirdre peered down at the strange snail that was now sniffing the goo tentatively.

"A Carnivorous Peruvian Gnashing Snail," said Uncle Dilbert affectionately. "Eats anything and I mean anything. Gotta be careful how you handle these or they'll take your hand off."

"Really?" Deirdre took an involuntary step backwards from the snail.

"Well, a few fingers at least," said Uncle Dilbert consolingly, "maybe not the whole hand."

The snail sniffed the goo several more times before leaping high into the air, pirouetting like a prima ballerina, then diving headfirst down into the slime. It began to chomp its way through it like it was the most delicious treat in the world, its jaws opening wider than Deirdre would have thought possible.

"Will it eat it all?" she asked.

"I should think so," Uncle Dilbert replied, "he's not been fed for a few weeks so he's pretty hungry."

They were just leaving the soon-to-be goo-free toilets when there came a loud, resounding gong that echoed throughout the entire house.

"Dinnertime," said Deirdre, "posh one too, Mum says. Monsieur Volcan's trying out some new dishes, are you coming?"

"Try and stop me," Uncle Dilbert smacked his

lips noisily at the thought, "just let me change into something more… appropriate…" He clicked his fingers once and his scruffy, dirt-stained blue overalls vanished — to be replaced by nothing but a pair of florescent yellow and green Bermuda shorts. Uncle Dilbert shrieked at his near-nakedness and clicked his fingers once more. The Bermuda shorts disappeared and in their place was a long, flowing, bright-pink ballgown with garish frills and puffy shoulders.

Deirdre doubled over with laughter as Uncle Dilbert, catching sight of himself in the large bathroom mirror, first yelled in horror and then stopped to admire the excellent job his spell had worked on his bright red lipstick. "Quite flattering…" he mumbled with a quick pout. One more click of the fingers and he found himself dressed in a formal tuxedo jacket, a crisp white shirt with a black bowtie and a fine silken cummerbund around his podgy middle. All traces of makeup were gone, as was his red and gold bandana. His normally wiry black hair had been magically slicked back into a neat coiffure that coincidentally covered his large bald spot. He admired himself in the mirror, grinned at his reflection and walked smugly out into the corridor. Deirdre followed, still sniggering.

"Uncle Bert?" she said, desperately trying to hide her giggles. Uncle Dilbert turned around. Deirdre pointed to his bare and extremely hairy knees which were gloriously on show thanks to the familiar Bermuda shorts he had conjured to go with his black tie and tails. For a minute he looked like he might explode with anger. Then his face fell in defeat, he sighed loudly and said, "Oh that'll have to do. Come on then."

He led the way down the corridor. Deirdre skipped up to meet him and put her hand in his. "Uncle Dilbert..."

"What?"

"Are there wizards at Grimley Academy?"

"A few," he shrugged. "Most of them go somewhere else."

CHAPTER 4
THE HEAD CHEF

The Darklys gathered downstairs in the family dining hall and sat down around a large and immaculately set table. Already waiting were Mr and Mrs Darkly, Grandpa Horace, Grandma Hortense and baby Errol, who gurgled and drooled happily in his highchair. All of the family were dressed in their smartest clothes and there was a definite air of apprehension amongst them. Deirdre knew all of this was for the benefit of their temperamental Head Chef, who was a stickler for perfection. They were eating with the finest silver on the finest bone-china and drinking from crystal wine glasses. The hundreds of candles that hung from the great chandelier in the centre of the ceiling were all lit and cast a dim, shadowy glow upon proceedings below.

Deirdre and Uncle Dilbert were the last to arrive and sat themselves down on two empty chairs. "Here they are," said Mr Darkly jovially and with ill-hidden relief, "we thought you weren't coming!"

"Just finished cleaning up the third-floor toilets," said Uncle Dilbert, "with the help of my glamorous assistant here." He winked at Deirdre.

"What are you wearing?" asked Mrs Darkly, looking in disbelief at Dilbert's highly original black-tie and Bermuda shorts combination.

He sniffed haughtily and sat down. "Just thought I'd try something a little different." Mrs Darkly gave him a familiar look that said 'your magic went wrong again, didn't it...?' "Well," Uncle Dilbert retorted, even though Mrs Darkly hadn't actually said anything out loud, "no-one can see anyway, look," he gestured to his lower half, "I'm half hidden underneath the table!"

"Well you can just stay that way," Mrs Darkly looked half- reproving and half-amused. "Auguste has gone to a lot of trouble this evening."

"Who's looking after the guests?" asked Deirdre, thinking of all the hungry Fright Folk in the guest dining hall where Monsieur Volcan usually held court.

"Wilhelmina is," said Mr Darkly, glancing surreptitiously at his wife. As if on cue there came a short, shrill shriek followed by the almighty clatter of broken crockery and clanging cutlery. Next came the groans and grumbles of several severely soup-sodden spooks.

The doors to the dining room opened and in hobbled a small hunchback dressed in a white apron, a tall chef's hat and pushing a large trolley laden with several covered serving dishes. "Thank you Raymond," said Mr Darkly. Raymond grunted and hobbled back to the kitchen. "Now," Mr Darkly continued, "as we are all dressed for dinner, I think it is only appropriate that we dress for dinner." There was muttered agreement at this proposition. All of a sudden, four out of the seven sitting at the dining-room table transformed into four rather different-looking creatures.

Mr Darkly's face drained of all colour, becoming a greyish purple. Dark shadows hung under his eyes, which were wide and bloodshot. His hands turned the same colour as his face and his nails grew yellow and pointed. His clothes didn't alter; he still wore the same garish stripy tank top and large bowtie. Mr Darkly became, perhaps, the most colourful vampire you have ever seen (if you have seen one at all).

Mrs Darkly's skin turned a vivid dark-green, and several large warts appeared on her face. Even as a witch, she was still quite as pretty as when she was Camouflaged, despite her nose being bigger and slightly more crooked. Her hair turned even darker black and frizzier and her nails much longer and sharper.

In place of Grandpa Horace there now sat a great, hairy creature covered in greying brown fur. It had a long snout with a large wet black nose at the end of it and long, sharp claws sticking out from furry hands. He was getting on in years and the row of huge and scary-looking sharp teeth were actually false fangs that he took out and put in a glass of water by his bed each night. In his Typical form, Grandpa Horace had no hair at all on the top of his head but enough in his ears and nostrils to make up for it. In his werewolf state he was covered in nothing but, and had no reason at all to complain about the cold drafts that sometimes rattled through Darkly Manor.

Grandma Hortense wasn't there at all! Her reading glasses floated in mid-air, together with a large brown hearing-aid, a purple knitted hat and the rest of her clothes. Her knitting needles clicked and clacked in her invisible hands as she waited for dinner to be served; Grandma Hortense could knit Mr Darkly a new tank top quicker than you or I could go out and buy one. Not that we would buy one — they were mostly horrid — but Mr Darkly had, over the years, learned to love them.

Deirdre picked up her soup spoon and twirled it absentmindedly in her now clawed hands. She had to kick off her shoes before dropping her Camouflage because her large, clawed gargoyle feet would not fit into them. It had taken many a telling-off from her mother and many more trips to L. J. Silver's Shoe Superstore before she had acquired the habit. A gargoyle, for those of you who don't know, is a bit like an overgrown bat, except that gargoyle wings are on their back rather than their arms. In her natural state, Deirdre's skin became rougher and turned a nut-brown colour, and her face had a more beaky, bird-like appearance to it. Her hair was no longer tied up in bunches; it had grown wilder and more mane-like. The bobbles that normally tamed it had a habit of flying off in opposite directions whenever she transformed. Just as she would automatically kick her shoes off before dropping Camouflage, her family had instinctively learned to duck. If you weren't fast enough, you paid the price (just ask Uncle Dilbert about the time he had to wear an eye-patch for three weeks).

Deirdre shifted uncomfortably in her seat as her long, prehensile tail flopped over the back of her chair, and she gave her large, leathery bat-like wings a few quick flaps to stretch them. There was a collective sigh of relief as the Darkly family adopted their natural states. Being Camouflaged for too long could be quite a strain for monsters and dropping one's Camouflage was like slipping into a warm bath after a long, cold walk in the rain.

Uncle Dilbert, as a wizard, did not need Camouflage. After all, any old man with a beard could claim to be a wizard and, likewise, any old wizard with a beard could claim to be a man. He was, at that moment, eyeing the dishes with an even hungrier expression on his pudgy face than usual. "When can we eat?"

"When Monsieur Volcan arrives," said Mrs Darkly sternly, "and not a moment before! Ah, here he comes."

The door burst open once again, and this time in walked a tall, gaunt zombie dressed impeccably in bowtie and tails and carrying a covered tray. He marched over to the Darklys, bowed slightly and placed the tray gently on the table. The family looked at it expectantly as the Maitre D' lifted the lid with a flourish of his white-gloved hand.

"Bonjour!" bellowed the severed head of Auguste Volcan, Head Chef and supreme connoisseur of cordon-bleu. In his youth, Auguste Volcan had been the Head Chef in the court of King Louis XIV. However, he was accused of trying to poison the king and sentenced to death by beheading when he tried out a new recipe that involved artichoke hearts, garlic butter, smoked salmon, dried pondweed and beetles guts. He survived (well, his head did) after a warlock friend of his intervened, stole the head from the executioner's basket and brought it back to life again. Quite why Monsieur Volcan's warlock friend couldn't stop the beheading in the first place, we shall probably never know for sure. After extensive research, however, I have good reason to believe that said warlock was heavily involved in a snakes and ladders tournament that day and completely lost track of time.

This also goes some way to explaining why he didn't think to steal Monsieur Volcan's body along with his head.

Despite being just a head, Monsieur Volcan took great pride in his appearance. His hair was a flaming red as fiery as his temper and was usually held in a neat coiffure underneath his white chef's hat. Tonight, however, he wore a smart black beret and a purple silk neckerchief and his thin, bristly moustache was waxed to curl upwards at each end. It was Alphonse the zombie Maitre D's duty to keep it freshly waxed, as well as attend to any other difficulties a living head separated from its body might have. Wiping a runny nose, for example, scratching an itch, or having a hand to cough in when something tickled his throat.

"Are we prepared tonight for culinary perfection?" The Darklys all murmured their approval at once. "For each of you," the Head Chef continued, "I have prepared an individual starter, an individual main course and an individual dessert. If you enjoy I shall introduce these dishes to my kitchen. Allez!" he rolled his eyes up to Alphonse, who at once lifted him over each of the starters.

"For the hungry vampire," he gestured to Mr Darkly, "I have prepared oxtail and goat's-blood soup with fresh rolls followed by mammoth-steak, rare, of course, with a crushed cockroach sauce."

"For the hag," he motioned over to Mrs Darkly and Alphonse obediently carried him over, "we have black slugs sautéed in their own slime followed by squid tentacles in nettle gravy."

"For little baby Errol, I have prepared mashed

beetle innards and earthworms with a side of cauliflower. I do not mind if he does not like the cauliflower."

"For the warlock on the go," Alphonse moved him over to Uncle Dilbert, "newt's eyes on fried bread followed by live eel pie." Uncle Dilbert smacked his lips and made to dive straight in to his eel pie but stopped short at a look from his sister.

"For the Grandparents, who struggle with the tough food, I make things nice and plain. For the werewolf with false fangs I make a bowl of black- rat stew, very little chewing involved. And for the invisible lady," Alphonse removed the lid from the tray to reveal well, nothing. "I make for you an invisible salad. I have been experimenting with invisibility in my kitchen for several months — half my staff disappeared in the process — but finally, voila! It is a surprise with every bite, a mystery meal your guests will love. Incidentally, try not to let too many ingredients slither away."

"And, finally, for the little gargoyle," Alphonse removed Deirdre's tray lid, "tarantula legs with a spicy weasel-brain sauce followed by grilled armadillo smothered in maggots." Now I know what you're thinking: how can Deirdre have a tarantula for a pet and then go and eat tarantula legs? Well, not all tarantulas talked, of course, and those that did could tell Head Chefs not to cook them.

Monsieur Volcan looked proudly down at his delicious creations, each one a culinary masterpiece. "Bon appetit!" he bellowed before Alphonse whisked him away back to his kitchen. The Darklys wasted no time in tucking in and there was hardly a noise to be heard save for greedy gulps and slurps and the gentle chinking of cutlery on china. After several minutes Mrs Darkly spoke, "So the third-floor toilet's fixed now, is it?"

"Course it is," said Uncle Dilbert, slurping a wiggling eel tail into his mouth like it was a strand of spaghetti. "You know me Sis, no job too messy…"

"What do you think it was," asked Mr Darkly, "all that slime?"

"Probably those spectre twins in room 304," said Dilbert.

"Ha!" laughed Grandma Hortense. "Dive-bombing the toilets like old Ogden Goop used to at school. Remember him, Horace?"

Grandpa Horace chuckled, "Flooded the whole of the science labs with his ectoplasm; I remember we got to go home early. Good old Ogden was a hero for that."

"You'll have all that to come, Deirdre, when you go to Grimley Academy," said Grandma Hortense. "Mummies lassoing you in the corridors with their bandages, vampires dropping down at you unexpectedly from the ceiling. Zombie lads juggling with their own body parts—"

"Show-offs," muttered Grandpa Horace.

"Oh," Grandma Hortense huffed, "and I suppose you weren't when you entered yourself into the Fifth Year Talent Contest with your juggling act!"

Grandpa Horace shifted slightly in his seat. "Some say I missed my calling."

"That's not all you missed," said Grandma Hortense.

"I didn't know you could juggle, Grandpa," said Deirdre.

"He can't!" Grandma Hortense snorted, "He tried, though, with three griffin eggs, would you believe."

"What happened?" asked Deirdre.

"He dropped them of course!" said Grandma Hortense, "Egg yolk all over him — he was the laughing stock of the school for the rest of term."

"I only dropped two," said Grandpa Horace defensively.

"What happened to the other one?" asked Deirdre through a mouthful of grilled armadillo.

"The other one hatched, that's what," said Grandma Hortense, "hatched and started flying around the hall screeching blue murder. I tell you, a room full of school pupils and a frightened grifflet do not mix. Our uniforms smelled terrible for weeks after."

"End of term soon though," said Mrs Darkly, moving the conversation on to more savoury topics. "You'll be eleven years old in three weeks, Deirdre. Have you thought what you'd like for your birthday this year?" her mother asked, wiping Errol's face with his bib.

Deirdre, as it happens, had completely forgotten about her birthday. She thought for a few seconds then said, "I might like a new bag for school, I think. I expect I'll have lots more books and things for Grimley Academy."

"Is that it?" said Uncle Dilbert, "A bag? Blimey Deirdre, a girl your age should have a list a mile long. Tell you what, seeing as it's Saturday tomorrow, you and me'll go into the village and you can pick out some stuff this lot can buy you," he said, gesturing with his head to the rest of the family and spraying the table with droplets of eel blood in the process. "Bring Bogby if you like, that way I can slip off to the Drunken Monk for a swift half with Ebeneezer if my feet get tired."

The rest of the meal passed pleasantly enough and when Monsieur Volcan returned they praised his culinary genius warmly, and he went away a very happy head indeed. Deirdre went upstairs not long afterward, brushed her teeth and got ready for bed before saying goodnight to her family. She read one of her favourite books for a while: Grim Scarytales for Ghouls and Boils of all Ages by Confucius Gout. She was enjoying a rather exciting story about Bertram the Bald Bogeyman, who saved the court of King Brian XII from an infestation of man-eating giraffes, before she finally drifted off to sleep.

"Alright Deedee?" Said Bogby coolly as he reached
the bottom of the wooden stairs.

CHAPTER 5
THE CREATURES FROM THE BLACK'S LAGOON

Deirdre usually stayed in bed on a Saturday, but today she awoke bright and early. Uncle Dilbert, after last night's gastronomic excesses, was still snoring like a hippopotamus with a blocked nose even after she had washed, dressed, had breakfast and was ready to go.

"You go on without me," he grunted, rolling over and pulling the duvet over his head, "I'll catch you up..."

And so Deirdre made her way out of Darkly Manor without her uncle, along the gravel drive and into the village of Grimley-by-the-Sea. She was determined to pick out the biggest, most expensive present she could find for her Uncle Dilbert to buy her. Instead of heading straight to the high street she took a detour down a rocky path that wended its way to a large and very murky lagoon. A lagoon, as I'm sure you already know, is a stretch of salt water that is partially separated from the sea. This particular lagoon was connected via underwater tunnels to the vast ocean beyond the cliffs, and every now and again a stray hammerhead shark or giant shrieking eel would find its way through. Here and there, bubbles erupted ominously on the dark surface. Great clumps of weeds sat amongst rocks that protruded at strange angles. Deirdre walked purposefully over to a pole that had a sign nailed to the top of it and a small bell hanging down. The sign read:

> *Mr and Mrs P. Black.*
>
> *Please ring for assistance.*

Deirdre rang the bell a few times then waited. After a few seconds there came a huge eruption of bubbles, as if a thousand small fish had all decided to blow raspberries at once. It was followed by a squelching sound as what looked like a giant, pink and squishy path leading from the bank to the small island emerged from beneath the lagoon. Deirdre wasted no time in hopping smartly on to the slimy bridge and making her way to the island, as she had done so many times before. She made her way to the centre of the lagoon toward a strange, oddly shaped pile of wood heaped together on a small and mossy island. It was the wrecked remains of a large upside-down galleon sitting quite comfortably on the back of a giant squid: it was also home to the Black family. The squid was extremely tame and, what's more, very old and tired. It hardly moved at all, preferring to spend most of its time asleep (though it did sometimes cough or sneeze, sending any unprepared dwellers inside flying gills over tail).

Walking along a gigantic, slimy tentacle took some getting used to, but Deirdre had become quite an expert and she didn't slip once. As soon as she stepped on to the squid's springy head, the tentacle disappeared back beneath the dark water with a loud gloop and she knocked on the wooden door. It was opened soon after by a sullen-faced creature, slightly taller than Deirdre, wearing jeans and a sparkly pink t-shirt. Her skin was a dark, mottled green and she had two large fins sticking out of either side of her head. Another fin ran from the top of her head down almost to the tip of her crocodile-like tail, and her fingers and toes were long and webbed. Her long, lank hair hung messily about her head. Her mouth was wide, with thick, dark-green lips and two rows of large, pointed teeth. It was currently set in a sneer as her bulbous black eyes stared down at Deirdre.

"Hi Pondalina," said Deirdre, "is☐" Pondalina turned her head and bellowed unceremoniously:

"BOGBY! IT'S DEIRDRE!" She turned back to Deirdre, "You'd better come in," and sloped back indoors. Deirdre followed.

The Black family had adapted their upside-down ship very nicely indeed and it almost resembled an average home.

Except it was wetter.

Much wetter.

And darker.

And had far more living things hidden inside it than any house should have.

Then there was the constant sound of dripping. The damp moss that grew almost everywhere dripped non-stop all day and all night into the five-inch-thick mud and water that covered the floor. The furniture was constantly damp. The only light came from the luminous plants that lined the walls. Deirdre felt sure that there were several new species of pond life and at least three large eels living undiscovered in the ankle-high sludge. However, damp, cold and murky was to the Blacks as a roaring fire and a steaming mug of hot cocoa with marshmallows is to you or I.

"Ah, good morning Deirdre," said Mr Black, as Deirdre entered the living room. A tall, thin creature, he was almost exactly like his eldest child Pondalina except for the glasses perched on his face, the thick pondweed moustache above his top lip and the fact that he was actually smiling.

"Good morning, Mr Black," Deirdre replied politely.

"Come, come now, Deirdre," said Mr Black smiling and showing almost every one of his long, sharp teeth. "You've known us long enough now. It's Peat," he said gesturing to himself, "and Marsha," and then to Mrs Black, who had just that moment entered the room. She was a little shorter than her husband and, like her daughter's, her pondweed hair fell down her back (though hers was neater and tied up in a ponytail). Deirdre smiled at Mr and Mrs Black, unsure of what to say next, and silently resolved never to start calling them by their first names.

"Bogby will be down in a minute, Deirdre," said Mrs Black, sitting down with a squelch in an armchair. She unfolded today's copy of The Grimley Gazette, while Mr Black (whistling merrily) began tidying the breakfast things away. "Won't you take a seat?" Deirdre looked tentatively at the sopping sofa and, unseen, surreptitiously gave it a quick prod with her pointed tail; not wishing to appear rude she made to sit down. She was saved by the appearance of the smallest Black, making his way casually down the stairs. Bogby looked practically identical to the others, but he wore his head-fin Mohican style. He wore a scruffy, black t-shirt advertising his favourite band — The Spearfish. His tatty, old jeans sported some severe rips and slashes, and were decorated with several fishing hooks and colourful lures.

"Alright Deedee?" said Bogby coolly, as he reached the bottom of the wooden stairs.

"Great thanks," said Deirdre, relieved she wouldn't have to walk around all day with a wet bottom.

"We're off out, Mum," said Bogby grabbing his rucksack, "I'll grab some lunch in the village so Dad doesn't have to make me anything."

"Okay son," said Mrs Black, giving him a kiss on the cheek, "have a good day. Bye Deirdre."

The two of them rang the bell then made their way back across the slippery squid tentacle and off into the village.

CHAPTER 6
THE DRUNKEN MONK

As it was still quite early, the village was not yet hustling and bustling like it usually was. Deirdre and Bogby made their way down Bleakly Lane, the main street, stopping every now and again to look inside a particularly interesting shop window. Inside Moreau's Monstrous Menagerie there was a selection of sabre-toothed gerbils gnawing hungrily on their cages while multi-coloured Paracreeps (a rather ugly cross of parakeet and tarantula) scuttled and flapped along the ceiling. Mad Hattie's Manic Mansion, the most dangerous practical joke shop in Grimley, proclaimed a sale on snapping toilet seats and Diarrhoea Dog-Biscuits — A Complete Carpet Catastrophe for just 50p (WARNING: RESULTS ARE INSTANT — ONLY USE ON ENEMIES)! They passed by Granny Witherspoon's Olde Time Sweet Shoppe with its walls of gingerbread, windows of clear sugar, floors of boiled sweets and roof of thick, white icing.

"Do you want to go in?" asked Bogby, slowing down and gesturing through the door with a webbed hand.

"Not really," said Deirdre. "It's a bit old-fashioned, don't you think? They sell all the old sweets like Mint Scumbugs and Chocolate Slimes and things. We can go to Chuckleby's instead if you want?" Bogby shrugged and shuffled after her. To tell the truth Deirdre always had a strange, uneasy feeling about Granny Witherspoon's Olde Time Sweet Shoppe. She couldn't quite put her finger on it but there was something about children and gingerbread houses that did not mix.

As they made their way down the Lane they saw more and more shopkeepers attempting to promote their wares and services. A sign outside Mr Todd's Barbershop read: 'Our prices slashed, NOT your throat!' C. J. Hook's Second-Hand Shop had a special offer on broken alarm clocks and outside a small shop called Elvira's Evil Emporium there was a sign that read: 'Do you dread drizzle? Are you in constant fear of flash floods? Does water of any kind ruin more than your delicates? Then try Elvira's patented All-in-One All-Over Fully Waterproof Macintosh ON SALE NOW at only 29.99 and say $\underline{NO}$ to H_2O today!'

The pair passed by several bookshops on their way down the lane. The biggest and most ominous-looking of these was called Stonywarts, but Deirdre and Bogby never went in there. It was run by Emmeline Pebble, a grumpy, hunchbacked old dwarf who was famous throughout all Grimley for her terrible moods and tendency to insult her poor staff behind their backs for no reason whatsoever. They went instead to a much smaller bookshop called Madame LeFey's and went in. The small bookshop received no light from the sunny street outside (well, as sunny as it gets in Grimley-by-the-Sea), but odd candles flickered here and there casting what little light they could. Madame LeFey's was exactly what a bookshop should be — dim and musty and with a real air of expectancy that just around the corner you might find something *really* special. A genuine treasure map hidden behind a shelf for example, or a book that contained a real genie trapped within its pages (which, Deirdre had heard, *had* actually happened once). The books were also as books should be, overflowing from their sections and spilling out from the shelves into piles on the ground and on to every flat surface that could hold them. Tables, chairs, windowsills, a passing gremlin customer's oddly flat head. There was little else in the way of furniture in Madame LeFey's save for a moth-eaten old armchair and a battered desk, on top of which sat an old till with a few paltry coins inside.

Deirdre found herself looking up at a large bookcase in a gloomy corner where a tattered old label on a high shelf read - 'Local History'. Deirdre leaned in closer to the books directly in front of her and read some of the titles out loud.

"The Grimley Gazette — 1532-1790: A History of Horrors by Arctorus Bilge... Notable Ghosts of Grimley by Morgana Fennimore... Poltergeists Past and Present by Pomeroy Potts... The Great Vampiric Families of Grimley-by-the-Sea by Vladimir Fiendish...

"See anything you like, dearies?" Deirdre and Bogby both jumped as Madame LeFey appeared next to them with a small pop accompanied by a puff of smoke. She was dressed in what looked like an old and very tattered wedding dress, the hem of which was hovering some way off the dusty floor — as was Madame LeFey.

"Just browsing thanks," said Bogby.

"Right you are," trilled Madame LeFey, and as quickly as she had appeared she disappeared with the same pop and puff of smoke.

Deirdre walked over to a section labelled 'Reference' and plucked out *A Frightologist's Field Guide* by Archibald Bott. It was subtitled *A Complete Guide To*

Fright Folk of the World, Their Habits, Homes and Behaviour.

"What's that?" asked Bogby, sloping over.

"It's a book Grandpa Horace is always going on about," Deirdre replied, "he says it's a textbook at Grimley Academy."

She flicked a few pages and saw that it was a vast encyclopaedia of all known Fright Folk and other non-Typical beings. In the few pages she flicked through she saw entries for sea creatures, swamp creatures, trolls and ogres, giants, snow creatures, night creatures, demons and more. There were sections on where certain creatures could be found, how to tell different species apart, as well as a section on Fright Folk from other countries. These included chimaeras, gorgons, centaurs, minotaurs, sirens and harpies and even a section on *Mythical Creatures*, such as leprechauns, genies, fairies and pixies. She couldn't resist turning to the heading marked 'Gargoyle', and read:

GARGOYLE
(GROTESQUIEM FLAPPIUS)

The common **GARGOYLE** is a relative of the VAMPIRE (NOSFERATUS SANGUIS) family but, instead of the ability to transform into a secondary flying mammal, the **GARGOYLE** has its own set of fully operational wings when in its natural state. An extremely prehensile beast (PREHENSILE (adj) — adapted for seizing or grasping), the **GARGOYLE'S** clawed hands and feet allow it to climb objects with ease and cling to surfaces for extended periods without the need to hover. The **GARGOYLE** can fly for many miles before tiring and is capable of great feats of athleticism, for its body is aerodynamic in build and its bones are light and hollow like a bird's. Nocturnal by habit, the first **GARGOYLES** found themselves most at home in high, shadowy places such as cliff-top caves, cathedral rooftops and belfries. This helped propagate the myth that stone carvings of them were used by early **TYPICAL** churchgoers to ward off evil spirits. They were, in fact, merely sleeping somewhere far out of the way of the **TYPICALS** that plagued them. Famous **GARGOYLES** of note include: Lady Felicity Pennyfeather — the first gargoyle to fly over the Atlantic unaided, General-Brigadier Bambridge Hawke — decorated war hero, and Professor Sir Flagstaff Swyft II — noted explorer and discoverer of the Stripy Rotgobbler. Unfortunately, as Professor Swyft found out too late, the Stripy Rotgobbler's primary food source is the **GARGOYLE**. All that was left of him after this encounter was a pair of spectacles, a pith helmet and a notebook in which were written the words - "Help me! Help me! It's eating my legs! I think I'll name it the Stripy Rotgobbler. And please someone tell my wife I always hated her cooking."

As most often happens in books of this nature, Deirdre found that each fascinating section she read led her to yet another section. She flicked over to the 'T' section for 'Typical' and read:

TYPICAL
(NORMALICUS BORINGIVUM)

A **TYPICAL** is a being without any form of supernatural abilities or powers. These individuals often live a life completely oblivious to the true existence of **FRIGHT FOLK**, placing them in the category of **FAIRYTALE** or mere **SUPERSTITION**. Altogether not a very bright race.

They browsed at books for a good while before Deirdre decided she would like The Frightologist's Field Guide for her birthday. She asked Madame LeFey if she could set it aside which she said she was more than happy to do. They left and turned down Pitiable Way, making a dash past Toadblatt's Tonics and Philtres where they had to dodge around a swirling purple mist that was gushing out of there with alarming speed. The streets were beginning to fill up now and Deirdre and Bogby decided to get something to eat before it became too busy. They decided to eat at Lumpy's, which was an older and less popular chain of fast-food restaurant. Deirdre and Bogby both liked eating there, the food was much better than at Sergeant Sopwith's Squid Stall, or Mrs Mump's Miscellaneous Mixed Grill. At Lumpy's you always knew you were in for a good meal, as opposed to Mrs Mump's where you never really knew what the meal on your plate was. Or had ever been. Lumpy's had been founded centuries earlier by a wandering minstrel named Sir Lumpo and when it had first opened it was known as Sir Lumpo's Mammoth-Steak and Ale Hut. Sir Lumpo had been famous for his constantly runny nose and severe lack of taste buds. How fitting then that his should become the first ever Fright Folk fast-food restaurant.

Bogby had a toadburger, a portion of flies and a chocolate mudshake; Deirdre had the rat-wraps with a strawberry mudshake. At about half-past twelve they decided to see if Uncle Dilbert had managed to crawl out of bed and so went to the one place in all of Grimley-by-the-Sea he would be. They made their way down to a place called Unruly Row.

Unruly Row was famous in Grimley for being the worst place to find yourself alone at night, or even the daytime. In fact, just not going there at all — ever — was generally good advice. There were several pubs and inns in this part of town and each one was grimier and smellier than the last. The Rancid Toenail was run by an angry goblin named Wickersnuck, who was so antisocial he had never actually let anyone in. He would open the place every day at the same time and the moment anyone even put a claw inside the door, he would chase them out, screaming at the top of his voice. He had so far only staved off starvation by eating whatever he found in his nose and drinking his own armpit sweat. The Badger's Brain pub wasn't much better. The landlady was a particularly fearsome female bigfoot named Fairly Feral Beryl, who had a nasty habit of biting the heads off customers who were late paying their tab. Or if they were late turning up for the pub opening. Or if they were late waking up that morning. Or even if they slurped their drinks a little too loudly. You would think that this would be bad for business — not so. The Badger's Brain served the finest earwig-mucus lasagne in Grimley-by-the-Sea. It was so good, it was worth having your head bitten off.

Deirdre and Bogby made their way to Uncle Dilbert's favourite pub, The Drunken Monk, and went inside. It was a dark and smoky place. Several hags and a vampire played cards in a dark corner, while a decaying mummy and a zombie discussed the price of bandages over two steaming tankards of a frothy green liquid. Unsurprisingly, they found Uncle Dilbert sitting in another smoky corner. In fact, all the corners of The

Drunken Monk appeared to be smoky. This had nothing to do with the Fright Folk inside smoking cigarettes or pipes. Monsters aren't that stupid. It was left over from the many phantoms, wizards and hags who enjoyed appearing and disappearing in clouds of smoke whenever the mood took them. Uncle Dilbert was chatting with old Ebeneezer McSwiggin, the ghost landlord. McSwiggin had once been a ferocious pirate captain whose ship, also called The Drunken Monk (he was a ferocious captain, not a very imaginative one), had run aground in Grimley hundreds of years ago. McSwiggin and his crew had been chasing a vicious giant squid when they found themselves in Grimley-by-the-Sea. For forty-six years Ebeneezer McSwiggin had chased that squid, across the seven seas and back again. He worked his crew almost to death in the chase. There was to be no rest, no food and no water until the beast was captured. It was his obsession, his one mission in life and no-one was going to take it from him. Until, that was, he was fired out of one of his own cannons by an angry (not to mention now rather elderly) cabin boy. When McSwiggin reappeared not long after as a ghost, it became clear he wasn't about to let a pesky little problem such as death stop his mad mission. The rest of his crew stopped celebrating the hilarious loss of their insane captain, and proceeded to fire themselves out of the cannons in a desperate attempt to get as far away from him as possible. It seems a shame to waste so much time in the pursuit of such a pointless task, unless, of course, your cause is just. Captain Ebeneezer McSwiggin's was just. JUST completely stupid and JUST a total waste of time. He claimed the squid had stolen his favourite set of dominoes. In actual fact the real thief was the ship's cat, Morris. McSwiggin's obituary in The Buccaneer's Bugle read:

Captain Ebeneezer Vivian McSwiggin: 1832-1901. Passionate pirate. Dedicated dominoes player. Stark, raving platypus-brained madman.

McSwiggin's ship is still in Grimley to this day. It is, in fact, now home to Bogby Black and his family. The giant squid on which it is perched hadn't always been so tame.

"Deirdre!" Uncle Dilbert bellowed, "Bogby lad! Come and join us!" They went over and joined them in their shadowy booth, but didn't sit down. "Ebeneezer," said Uncle Dilbert, "you remember my niece Deirdre and her friend Bogby?"

"Of course!" McSwiggin roared jovially. "Top o' the morning' to ye me buckos, what can I get ye?" He grinned at them flashing rows of blackened teeth. He had a shock of curly, grey hair that fell down to his shoulders and his beard was raggedy and unkempt. He wore a long captain's coat, knee-high boots, baggy pantaloons and a cutlass on his belt. He glared at them with his one good eye — although technically now he was dead he had no good eyes — but he glared at them all the same.

"I'll have a Cockroach-Cola please," said Deirdre.

"And I'll have a pond-weed and lemonade thanks," said Bogby.

"Oh," Deirdre added matter-of-factly, "and put them on Uncle Bert's tab, will you? It might teach him not to sleep in when he's promised his favourite niece he'd take her shopping for birthday presents."

McSwiggin cackled as he floated off to fetch the drinks. "I guess I had that coming didn't I?" said Uncle Dilbert. "Sorry Deirdre, it's just that I was up late playing darts with a couple of those travelling circus vampires we got staying at the hotel."

"Did you win?" asked Bogby with a dry smirk, or, in his case, a wet smirk.

"No," said Uncle Dilbert gloomily, "turns out they were the knife-throwing act. I didn't stand a chance. One of them kept putting their head against the dartboard, just below the spot the other was aiming for. He never missed!"

McSwiggin arrived a few minutes later with their drinks and joined them. While they drank he told them stories of all the exciting and dangerous things he had done as a pirate Captain. From swashbuckling tales of adventures on the high seas, to run-ins with man-eating sea creatures and bloody battles with barbaric buccaneers.

"Wow," said Deirdre in awe, after finishing her third Cockroach- Cola, "what an exciting life!"

"Aye," said McSwiggin, "but it's quite exciting being a landlord too," he looked rather gloomily around the room. "Why, just the other day I gave this werewolf fella the wrong change. Had a right laugh about it we did..." he tailed off. An awkward silence followed.

"Well," said Deirdre after a few uncomfortable

seconds, "we really should get going," she looked at Bogby and raised her eyebrows, "lots to do…"

They got up to leave amidst Uncle Dilbert's promises that he would catch up with them shortly and that his latest pint of Wyrd Brewe was his very last. Deirdre and Bogby looked at each other, rolled their eyes and left.

CHAPTER 7
MORTIMER

Leaving The Drunken Monk and Unruly Row altogether, they decided to take a walk down Miscellaneous Lane. The lane was a long row of shops that tailored for some of the more unusual inhabitants of Grimley-by-the-Sea. There were shops that created specialist outfits like jackets with extra sleeves and trousers with extra legs, as well as invisible clothing for invisible folk who didn't much like the idea of running around naked all day. There were also shops that would alter clothing as needed, perhaps adding slits for wings or a hole for a tail to fit through and so on. As they passed K. Midas and Sons: Quality Jewellers and rounded a corner they came across a group of young monsters. They were gathered in a circle and were all around Deirdre and Bogby's age. They were laughing and jeering and every now and again one of them would lunge into the middle as if to grab or poke something Deirdre couldn't quite see.

"Bone-head!" screeched one of the gang, a girl vampire with particularly buck-fangs.

"Skin-less freak!" yelled a zombie boy, his left eye flying out of its socket in his excitement and landing with a squelch on the pavement.

"Get back where you came from, bone-head!" cackled a small, shrill hag with warts all over her pointed nose.

"You used bone-head twice," said Deirdre walking over to them, Bogby staying some way behind her. "If you're going to be rude, ignorant scumbags, then at least be original rude, ignorant scumbags."

The gang stopped their tormenting and turned instead to Deirdre. "Well, well, well," said a posh voice from behind them all, "if it isn't Deirdre Darkly and her pet. Taking your fish for a walk, are you?"

"Hello Spectra," said Deirdre smiling, "you haven't left home without your pack of howler monkeys I see?"

Spectra Ghastly was the same age as Deirdre, a banshee with long, flowing silvery-white hair that she wore tied back in a ponytail. Her father was Hugo Ghastly, the Mayor of Grimley-by-the-Sea, which gave Spectra a heightened sense of her own importance and made her think she was a cut above everyone else. Deirdre had never been able to stand Spectra and, fortunately enough, the feeling was entirely mutual. Before Spectra could reply, however, there was a small scuffle followed by angry yells and Deirdre saw a small, hooded figure run off as fast as it could down the lane and out of sight.

"Aww," said Deirdre mockingly, "looks like your little victim ran away!"

Spectra's gang said nothing. They were quite a stupid bunch. Spectra herself, on the other hand, was an intelligent girl and — what's worse — an intelligent bully. An intelligent bully can boss other less intelligent bullies around and this is what Spectra did best. It wasn't easy being the cleverest out of a bunch of idiots. Spectra often found herself spending her time shouting at her gang for not having a brain between them. This was a problem constantly misinterpreted by young Edgar Cadaver, the zombie boy, who was forever taking his brain out and offering to share it around.

Poor old Edgar's brain, however, wasn't even big enough to make a very good paperweight, let alone share with others.

Spectra walked right up to Deirdre until they were almost nose to nose. "Listen, Darkly," she seethed, "I don't like you."

"Shame," said Deirdre in mock horror, "I think I'm in love with you!"

Bogby giggled and Spectra shot him a withering glare, "You can shut-up too, frog-FACE!" she shouted the last word in her deafening banshee scream. Poor Bogby was sent flying gills over tail and he landed in a pile of rotting vegetables thrown out by Cannibal Hector's Meat Feast Fast-Food Palace.

"You leave him out of this," said Deirdre, her eyes flashing dangerously.

"Or what?" Spectra smirked.

"Or I'll tell Daddy Dearest that his little princess is nothing but a great big stupid unimaginative bully."

"Ha!" Spectra screamed again, this time at Deirdre whose feet left the ground with the force of it. She managed to steady herself with her wings and landed gracefully. Spectra didn't like that one bit, she had much preferred Bogby's version of a swan-dive into some rubbish bins. "How about we settle this like monsters? You and me, a race around Grimley at midnight tonight. From the church steeple, round the lighthouse and back again. Loser becomes the other one's slave... for a week!"

"Deal!" said Deirdre, holding out her claw for Spectra to shake. Spectra took it with a pale hand and squeezed it as hard as she could. "See you at midnight," Spectra turned back to her gang, "and I'd bring a shovel and a pair of gloves if I were you; my horses need mucking out!" The howls of laughter from her gang echoed all down the alley.

"What is it with spoilt little rich girls and horses? I hate horses," said Deirdre testily as she and Bogby made their way to Chuckleby's Chocolate Box, "and I hate anyone who owns a horse." She was thinking, of course, about Millicent Parpington as well as Spectra Ghastly and how owning a horse seemed to make these two girls distinctly unbearable.

"What about jockeys?" said Bogby.

"Hate 'em!" said Deirdre.

"Highwaymen?"

"Hate 'em!"

"Cowboys?"

"Hate 'em worst of all!"

"Well what about centaurs, they're not really horses, are they?"

"Shut-up Bogby."

The only thing that could cheer Deirdre up now was some sugar-coated chocolatey goodness. They arrived at Chuckleby's just in time, as Bogby didn't think he could stand much more of Deirdre's bad mood. The owner, Mr Chuckleby, was half man and half hyena. He was known for his bright frilly shirts and garish bowties, which he always wore under a polka-dotted apron. He greeted them in his usual cheery way as they went inside.

It was no use, as Deirdre and Bogby knew full well, rushing your decision on something as important as sweets. They made their way slowly along the aisles of wicked treats, their mouths watering. They passed the Blood Blisters (realistic-looking blood-filled boils — adored by vampires), passed the Sugar Lice and Jelly Worms (that hopped *and* wriggled in the bag and in your stomach), ignored the huge jars of Rhubarb and Catsick, the Gelatine Skeletons and the Slime-filled Shrunken Heads and stopped at their respective favourites. Bogby eyed the huge display of Swamp-Chomps greedily and began counting out how many he could buy with the limited pocket money he had. Deirdre, on the other hand, had her eyes on a jumbo box of chocolate-covered Freakish Delight. It cost far too much for the jumbo box so, making a note to drop a few birthday hints to her family (Uncle Dilbert in particular), she and Bogby left the shop with their bags of Swamp-Chomps and Freakish Delight.

They had just rounded the corner that led back on to Bleakly Lane when they heard what sounded like a muffled sniff coming from behind some dustbins. They followed the sound until they found the source. It was a small boy wearing black, baggy trousers with silver chains on them and a black hooded top with the hood up over his head. His backpack lay on the floor next to him covered in badges and graffiti. A slogan scrawled in silver marker proclaimed: The Dead Heads Rule! They had only caught a fleeting glimpse of him earlier, but they both knew straight away that this was the boy Spectra Ghastly and her gang had been pushing around.

"Are you alright?" asked Deirdre peering, down at the boy.

With a start he looked up at them hastily, wiping

his face. "What do you want?" he snapped, his voice croaky from crying. "Haven't you bugged me enough?"

"That wasn't us," said Bogby pointedly, "we were the ones who distracted them long enough for you to get away!"

"Why were they bothering you like that?" asked Deirdre.

"Because of who I am," said the hooded boy, still sniffling.

"Well who are you?" asked Bogby.

"My name's M-Mortimer," he choked momentarily on a sob. Deirdre and Bogby looked at each other, neither one of them had ever heard of anyone famous, or *in*famous called Mortimer before. Deirdre was about to speak when Mortimer spoke again, "I'm the Grim Reaper's grandson." At that he pulled down his hood to reveal a skull-head devoid of any skin or hair. Two empty black sockets stared back at them and he bared his teeth in a ghoulish grin. "Well?" said Mortimer. "Aren't you going to run away screaming or throw stones through my eyeholes or something?"

Deirdre and Bogby looked at each other. Bogby held out his bag of Swamp-Chomps. "Want a sweet?"

CHAPTER 8
THE RACE

Deirdre and Bogby spent the rest of the day wandering around the village with their new friend Mortimer, talking and showing him the sights whilst getting to know him better. He was visiting Grimley with his grandfather, Death, from The Underworld where they both lived. Mortimer's parents had thought that it would be good for their only son to get out from the earth's core for once and accompany his grandfather on his business trip during the school holidays. Mortimer had been quite reluctant to go — quite rightly so, as being the Grandson of Death often attracts quite a lot of unwanted attention.

"So what's it like where you live, Mortimer?" asked Deirdre through the mouthful of Freakish Delight she was munching.

"Well," Mortimer replied through a similar mouthful, "there are huge bubbling lakes of molten lava, bottomless pits every few yards, unspeakably hideous creatures of the darkness every which way you turn and jagged razor-sharp rocks jutting out at you from every angle."

"Sounds lovely," said Deirdre.

"Oh, it is," said Mortimer, "it's quite nice here, though. I've never been around so many Fright Folk before. There's not many live in The Underworld save a few ratty old retired demons and some families of mole-people."

It turned out that Mortimer was — like Bogby and Deirdre — a fan of The Spearfish, but his favourite band was the skeletal Dead Heads. He and Bogby got into quite a heated discussion over the Dead Heads' latest album which was panned by critics.

"It was over-produced," said Bogby flatly, "too much going on all at once."

"They were experimenting," said Mortimer, "they had a couple of warlocks and witches on this one, throwing in a few sparks and whizzes."

"They should stick to what they know," said Bogby, "do what they do best."

"They were trying something different," said Mortimer, "they can't win!"

The argument was settled over a round of chocolate mudshakes and a large bag of Sneeze-and-Bunion flavoured crisps they bought from the General Store. This is where the ghoul on the go bought their groceries and other essentials. It was owned by a pair of rather grumpy old dwarfs with tattered old hats and long white beards named Walter and Sidney. (The dwarfs are named Walter and Sidney, not the tattered old hats and long white beards.) They strolled on past the library, which was run by a haggard old mummy named Mrs Figgis and her ghost parrot Eduardo. They crossed over to the Post Office because Mortimer had promised that he would send at least one postcard to his parents.

The Post Office was run by a very severe and efficient-looking centaur called Mrs de Canter. She clipped and clopped up and down all day barking (or should that be braying) orders to all of her poor staff and making sure her Post Office ran like clockwork. Deirdre was glad she didn't have Mrs de Canter for a teacher, for, as bad as Mrs Cowl was, she couldn't shout anywhere near as loud as the Post Mistress. Mortimer scribbled a quick hello on a postcard that read — 'Ghoulish Greetings From Grimley', addressed it to The Underworld and posted it before they all headed out again. They stopped at an old wooden ice-cream cart, the sign above which read: 'Mr Nippy's — the coldest ice-cream in the whole world!'

"Is that true?" said Mortimer to the yeti standing behind the cart.

"Certainly is," said the yeti proudly, "been in the family for years. I'm a twelfth generation Nippy! Our ice-cream is so cold it'll turn your eyes into icicles! It'll frost your face til you get face-freeze! It's so cold, it's colder than an Eskimo's nose. Course," he sniffed, "they prefer being called Inuits now. No idea about marketing... I mean, what rhymes with Inuit for crying out loud?" The three of them looked at each other as Mr Nippy the ice-cream-selling yeti mumbled to himself about the decline of the modern witty advertising slogan, before handing them three cones. "You want flakes with those?"

They all nodded. Mr Nippy reached behind the counter of his ice-cream cart and produced a large white plastic box labelled 'Dead Skin'. He grabbed a large handful and sprinkled liberally over all three ice-creams. With a 'thank you' the trio had one last look in Madame LeFey's and Chuckleby's before heading off home as it began to get dark. It turned out that Mortimer was staying at Darkly Manor so he and Deirdre said goodbye to Bogby and made their way up the gravel drive.

"So, what's your Grandad like...?" asked Deirdre tentatively as they approached the hotel.

"Well..." Mortimer thought for a moment, "he's great, really, he's always really nice to me and he's fun, but all everyone goes on about is the negative things about him."

"Like what?"

"Oh, like — 'he's the devourer of souls' and 'he's the lord of the undead', when really he's none of those things. He doesn't ever kill anyone, he just... moves them on."

Deirdre and Mortimer finished their sweets — before their tea, of course, you can't let your mealtimes spoil your appetite for sweets. They played in the attic with Kevin whilst listening to Deirdre's latest Spearfish record A Hook Through My Soul which they played on her gramophone. (A gramophone, for those of you that don't know, is a device that music was played on before stereos, CD players and computers. It was not, as you might think, a communication device for old ladies. That is a Granny-phone. The two are completely different things and must not be confused.)

As the evening wore on Mortimer told her more and more stories of his grandfather's past adventures. "This one time, he told me all about this ship he appeared on, the Marie something... I can't remember what it was called. Anyway, he hadn't been doing the job that long and he accidentally showed himself too early. Well, everybody started screaming their heads off, didn't they? They all leapt overboard, left their meals half-eaten, all their belongings behind, they didn't even lower the lifeboats!"

"Wow," said Deirdre, "I bet he never made that mistake again."

"Too right," said Mortimer, "he nearly got the sack for it. He carries this tattered old piece of paper around with him and when it's their time someone's name appears on it. When that happens he appears to them, shows them the scroll and then off they go! He just forgot to wait for the scroll that time, that's all." There was no sign of Mortimer's Grandad as they chatted in the lounge, but Mortimer wasn't surprised and explained to Deirdre that he usually kept himself to himself until his 'business' was all finished. "It's easier for him that way," said Mortimer yawning, "the more he keeps out of the way the quicker he gets done. I'd be surprised if we saw him at all the whole time we're here."

When bedtime rolled around they headed for the stairs together. Deirdre was just thinking about the comfortable bed and the good night's sleep waiting for her when Mortimer turned to her and whispered, "So, do you want me to come with you? Tonight, I mean?"

"What are you on about?" asked Deirdre.

"The race? With Spectra? I hid around the corner when I ran away from them and heard you both arrange it."

Deirdre's heart sank. How could she forget? The race, from the church steeple, round the lighthouse and back again at midnight tonight! All thoughts of her warm, comfortable bed vanished like a phantom in a cloud of smoke. "I'll meet you here at quarter to," she said trudging up to her room. "Don't fall asleep in the meantime."

At quarter to midnight Deirdre met Mortimer in the lounge as agreed. Both were very blurry-eyed — technically, Mortimer didn't have any eyes but he was still very sleepy. They snuck out easily enough, though it was a near miss when Wilhelmina nearly spotted them passing the guest dining hall as she was tidying up. Luckily, she slipped on a rogue grape that had escaped from a fruit salad and while she made the very short journey from mid-air to on the floor they ran out of the hotel.

"Do you think Bogby will meet us there?" asked Mortimer.

"I don't know," said Deirdre, who hoped her best friend would be there. She would feel an awful lot better about the whole thing if he was.

"Isn't that the way to his house?" said Mortimer. "Maybe we should go and see if he's waiting for us?"

"No need," came a familiar voice from a nearby clump of trees. Bogby stepped out of the shadows and into the faint moonlight. "Are we off then?" The three friends smiled at each other, Deirdre's spirits raised a little by Bogby's presence, and they made their way to the church.

The Church of St Ignatius was a huge, gothic building with almost as many twisted spires and missing roof tiles as Darkly Manor. Spectra and her cronies were already waiting by the huge bell tower. "I didn't think you were going to show up," she said, tapping her watch with a clawed finger.

"More like you were hoping I wasn't," said Deirdre.

Spectra smiled. "Are you ready then?" Deirdre nodded. "Right…" Spectra pulled out a piece of crisp green paper and handed it to Deirdre. "Sign this."

"What is it?" Deirdre took it and looked at it closely.

"It's a contract," Spectra smiled, "I've written it on official headed paper from my Father's office. That's a legal document so you can't get out of being my slave for a week when I win."

"Then you'd better sign it too," said Bogby, pointing a webbed finger at Spectra.

"I already have, bog-brain," Spectra scowled, "see?"

Deirdre held the paper up to the moonlight and saw that Spectra had indeed signed it at the bottom. "What do you think?"

Bogby and Mortimer scanned the paper. "It all seems above board to me," said Mortimer, "my dad works for The Underworld Administration and he brings home important documents all the time. It looks pretty official."

"I've even brought a pen," Spectra handed a large fountain pen over to Deirdre who took it and quickly scribbled her name at the bottom of the document next to Spectra's. "Good," Spectra smiled, "now I think Holly should keep hold of it until the race is over."

She went to hand the paper over to the buck-fanged vampire Holly Water but Deirdre grabbed her arm. "Wait! Who says you're in charge of the document?"

"I do because it was my idea, and from my father's office!" said Spectra.

"And what if I win?" said Deirdre. "She'll just rip it up and say it never existed. Or Harold will eat it."

All eyes fell on a particularly chubby mummy named Harold Sanders. "I will not!" he protested. His protestations might have been believable if at that moment his stomach hadn't made a noise like a ship's foghorn.

"Oh shove a bandage in it, Harold," Deirdre snapped. "Look, Holly holds one end and Bogby holds the other, agreed?"

Spectra looked indignant for a few moments before finally agreeing with a sharp nod of her head. "Right then," she said suddenly all business-like, "you know the rules?"

It was Deirdre's turn to nod sharply this time. "From the steeple, round the lighthouse and back again."

"Last one to put a claw on this roof loses," Spectra smirked, "I hope you like horses, Deirdre."

"Don't get her started," said Bogby rolling his eyes.

Deirdre and Spectra both flew up to the top of the crooked steeple and each placed one claw on the weathervane.

"Ready...?" said Holly from down below. Deirdre and Spectra said nothing but kept their eyes focused straight ahead. "Set...? GO!"

Before Deirdre could even push off from the steeple she felt a sharp elbow from Spectra catch her in

the ribs and knock the wind right out of her. She let go
of the steeple and toppled headfirst off the church roof,
righting herself just in time to land on the head of a
statue of St Ignatius himself. Wasting no time she took
a deep breath, muttered "Thanks Iggy," and pushed off
as hard as she could.

Spectra was quite a way ahead already, but
Deirdre's anger at her opponent's shocking display of
cheating spurred her on ever faster. The lighthouse was
past the outskirts of Grimley, high over the Monstrous
Mountains, over the cliff edge and out to sea. It was a
long way even if this was a leisurely flight on a sunny
afternoon. Racing your arch-nemesis at midnight when
you've already been elbowed in the ribs made it seem
like a flight to the moon and back.

The gap between them was closing all the time.
Deirdre flapped for all she was worth as they passed
over the village, shops and houses whizzing by in a
dark blur. They passed over the Black's Lagoon and
heard the giant squid snoring gently underneath the
water. Deirdre thought how nice it would be had it just
woken up for a moment, plucked Spectra Ghastly from
the air with one of its giant tentacles and swallowed her
whole.

But no such luck.

Deirdre's wings were flapping ten to the dozen,
her heart and lungs worked harder than they ever had
— and she was catching up. She saw Spectra turn her
head just for a moment and felt a jolt of delight as she
saw panic shoot across her face. They were high over
the Monstrous Mountains now and Deirdre heard what
sounded like low rumbles of thunder. Or was it the

giants and trolls snoring in their caves perhaps? Deirdre felt another jolt run through her, but it was nothing to do with delight this time. It was the thought of the bloodthirsty, terrifying creatures below that called those mountains home, and it was with no small relief that she passed over them. They were out across the village now. Below them candles still flickered in windows, but the only figure about was the lowly lamplighter snuffing out the streetlamps and whistling quietly to himself. Ahead of them now lay the steep cliff edge; below that was the dark ocean, which tonight lay unusually still and calm. Out ahead, but not yet visible, was the great lighthouse, surrounded by sharp, jagged rocks that even the slightest wave would crash upon, sending spray churning high into the air.

Deirdre put on a burst of speed, even though the pain in her wing-joints was excruciating — but there was no way that she was going to be beaten in a flying race by Spectra Ghastly. Especially when Spectra had cheated. They were almost level now, a strong sea breeze blew against them but Deirdre pushed ever onwards as the lighthouse came into view. To avoid any more dirty tricks, she kept away from Spectra — though made sure she could be seen creeping into the lead as they neared the great white lighthouse. Spectra was struggling against the wind and had not noticed Deirdre's progress. Unlike Deirdre, who had wings to hover with and a tail to steady her, Spectra had neither and she was being buffeted ever more violently. Deirdre felt grim satisfaction as she outstripped Spectra easily round the lighthouse and began the race for home. She passed Spectra, who shouted something that

Deirdre couldn't quite catch over the ever-increasing wind. She wasn't about to stop for a chat now: not when she was winning.

She was halfway back to the cliffs when she risked a glance behind her to see where Spectra was. As she turned around she saw that Spectra had just that moment rounded the lighthouse and was on her tail. She was still being battered by the wind quite a bit, but Deirdre wasn't going to hang around and watch. She turned back and, as she did so, heard an ear-splitting shriek carry on the wind. She turned instinctively and saw Spectra falling head over heels straight down towards the jagged rocks below.

Deirdre shot like an arrow towards her. She had no time to think, no time to decide whether the scream was fake or not. Spectra was falling faster than Deirdre was flying and the wind was tossing her around like a rag doll. Deirdre ignored the aches in her wing-joints and blinked away the stinging tears caused by the wind. Spectra was merely feet from the rocks now; so Deirdre knew that this was no trick — she was in real danger. Deirdre only had one chance. Swooping so low over the water that the spray soaked her to the skin, she caught Spectra awkwardly in her arms just as a colossal wave that would have swept them both away to sea broke over the lighthouse.

Spectra was sobbing and gasping for breath as Deirdre flew back towards the village. The flight back took a lot longer. They were both soaked through and even though the night wasn't particularly cold even the smallest breeze made them shiver. Deirdre was cold and exhausted and Spectra had not yet stopped crying.

As the church came into view, a small wave of relief came over her. It was almost over. She could just make out the others waiting for them on top of the roof when, without warning, Spectra leapt from her arms and flew off as fast as she could toward them. Deirdre was so shocked she gave chase immediately, all thoughts of the cold and weariness disappearing in an instant. All that mattered now was that she catch Spectra, as she could not be allowed to win. But she was still ahead and it looked like she was going to reach the steeple first, way ahead of Deirdre. One last push, one final burst of speed and Deirdre was almost level with her.

Almost…

Then Deirdre did some cheating of her own. Well, Spectra had cheated twice now so she had at least one dirty trick coming to her. Deirdre reached out a claw, grabbed Spectra's ankle and gave a sharp pull. Spectra flew spectacularly backwards through the air and past Deirdre, who used the momentum to shoot herself forwards. She landed gracefully on top of the steeple to the sound of rapturous applause and cheers from her friends.

Spectra Ghastly kicked and screamed and kicked some more at the 'injustice' of losing a race that she had cheated in.

CHAPTER 9
SLAVE FOR A WEEK

Spectra Ghastly kicked and screamed and kicked some more at the 'injustice' of losing a race that she had cheated in.

Twice.

But even her friends couldn't deny they had seen her elbow Deirdre at the start. And when Spectra herself couldn't think of any reasonable excuses for why she had been carried the entire way back, or why they were both soaking wet, it was decided that the victor was Deirdre.

"I'll see you Spectra!" Deirdre called after her as she, Bogby and Mortimer went in the opposite direction toward home. "Don't forget to bring a nice apron!"

"That was brilliant," said Bogby, who had not stopped grinning.

"Yeah," agreed Mortimer, "nice one Deirdre, that was some pretty fancy flying."

"Oh, it was nothing," said Deirdre, though she had to admit it was some pretty fancy flying.

"So what are you going to make her do?" asked Mortimer. He was particularly pleased that the ringleader of the bullies that had given him so much hassle was about to become a slave for a week.

Deirdre thought for a moment, "Hmmm... I'm not sure... There's always loads to do around the hotel. Mum and Dad are forever giving me jobs to do and I think it's time I had a week off. Besides, it's the summer holidays soon so I think I'll wait until then to make Spectra the newest maid in Darkly Manor!"

They were all still laughing and in very high spirits when they said goodbye to Bogby and reached the gravel drive that led to the front door.

"Normally I'd fly in through a window," said Deirdre, "but I don't think my wings would carry me, never mind the pair of us!" She flapped them gingerly and winced.

She and Mortimer crept through the front door, closed it as quietly as they could behind them and made their way across reception to the main staircase.

"Night then," said Mortimer as he reached the foot of the stairs, "and well done again, you really showed her."

"Thanks," Deirdre grinned, "it was —"

Suddenly there was a great, green flash and all the candles lit at once, filling the dark room with light. Deirdre and Mortimer squinted in the new brightness and, as her eyes adjusted, Deirdre's heart sank. There in the lounge were her mother, father and someone she didn't know dressed in a blue uniform.

"Well," said her mother in the breathy, high voice that Deirdre always associated with a telling-off. "It's very nice of you to drop by, Deirdre." Deirdre and Mortimer looked at each other, both at a loss for words. Fortunately, Mrs Darkly had enough words for everyone present. "Do you realise how worried we were? You weren't in your bed! There was no note, no explanation, no nothing! Where have you been?" Deirdre didn't even bother opening her mouth to protest. She knew from experience that any and all questions her mother may ask during a rant were merely rhetorical and not to be answered until she had let off steam. Perhaps in three or four weeks.

"We've been worried sick, Deirdre," said her father, "and you, Mortimer, your grandad was scared to… well, he was also very worried. He's out now looking for you both."

"We even called the police!" exclaimed Mrs Darkly. "Constable Barker here should arrest you both for wasting his time."

The overweight werewolf in blue stood to his paws and looked sternly down at Deirdre and Mortimer. He was tall, with greying fur on top of his head and a rather advanced middle-aged spread. He walked slowly toward the pair of them and talked even slower.

"Now then, you two have caused a lot of mischief this evening." Deirdre could practically hear Mortimer's knees knocking together. "You've given your family a real fright. I reckon the best thing to do now is send them both straight up off to bed. You have yourself a nice cup of tea Mr and Mrs Darkly, or something stronger if you've got it. It'll steady your nerves until morning and you can deal with these two then."

Deirdre and Mortimer climbed the stairs in silence and went straight to their rooms. All the glory Deirdre had felt just moments ago had vanished as quickly as an overweight cow in a piranha-filled stream. She got into her pyjamas, slumped into bed and tried to fall asleep as quickly as possible so she could forget all about this horrible night.

The next morning, however, things got off to a much worse start than Deirdre could have predicted.

As the Darklys were sitting down to breakfast amidst a rather frosty atmosphere, there came a smart rapping on the door. "Strange," said Mr Darkly as he got up to answer it, "we're not expecting any arrivals today. And whoever would call on a Sunday morning?"

Deirdre didn't quite know why, but she knew that whoever was at the door was something or someone to do with last night. And she was right. No sooner had Mr Darkly opened the door than in stormed none other than the Mayor of Grimley-by-the-Sea himself, Mr Hugo Ghastly. As if this wasn't bad enough, before him with head down and arms folded was his daughter Spectra Ghastly. Spectra looked as though she would rather be back falling headfirst into the sea again than in Darkly Manor on a Sunday morning.

"Mayor Ghastly...?" said Mr Darkly, quite at a loss for anything else to say. After all, how often does a Mayor come for breakfast?

"Hello Darkly," said Mayor Ghastly, a huge, walrus of a phantom with white, powdery skin and piggy little eyes. He was dressed in a smart, cream-coloured suit and bowtie and carried a thick cane. A huge, bushy white moustache that rivalled Uncle Dilbert's almost hid his entire mouth.

"Won't you come in...?" said Mr Darkly, almost bowing the Mayor inside. "Look dear, it's... the Mayor..."

Mrs Darkly nearly tipped over the entire breakfast table and all its contents in her eagerness to get to her feet. "Your Honour. What can we do for you, your Mayor-ship-ness... sir? Would you like some... toast?"

"Not for me, thank you Mrs Darkly," said Mayor Ghastly. "I'm afraid I — oh, is that Muttonchop's Maggot Marmalade you've got there? My favourite brand. Oh, go on then, just a slice, thanks." He let go of his daughter and helped himself to three slices of toast, over which he slathered the wriggling orange preserve before crunching noisily. "I'm afraid I'm here on some rather bad business…" he said, his mouth full and spraying tiny wriggling maggots all over the place (there were even some wriggling in his huge moustache — Deirdre thought they looked like tiny ramblers lost in a snow-covered forest). "Spectra here tells me," he continued, oblivious to the maggots' plight, "that young Deirdre challenged her to a race around the village last night. And, what's more, from the top of the church roof, around the lighthouse and back again."

Before anyone else had chance to speak, Deirdre had leapt to her feet partly succeeding where her mother had failed and knocking over the toast rack, the teapot and three cups, "That's not —"

"It's alright, Deirdre," the Mayor continued, "I got the truth out of her. I found this —" he pulled from inside his jacket pocket a familiar-looking sheet of green paper.

"What is it?" asked Mrs Darkly.

"It's a contract, Mrs Darkly," Mayor Ghastly continued, "written by my daughter on official headed paper and signed by her and Deirdre. It states that whoever loses said race will become the other's slave for one week."

Silence followed. Deirdre and Spectra glanced momentarily at each other before turning away again.

There was no point denying anything as it was all there for them to see in black and white. For a brief second Deirdre felt annoyed that Harold Sanders hadn't eaten the piece of paper.

"Slave for a week, eh?" said Mrs Darkly.

"What have you got to say for yourself, Deirdre?" said Mr Darkly.

Deirdre was silent for some time. "I won the race…?" Well, she might as well brag about her victory. It wasn't like she could get into any more trouble.

She was wrong.

After all the shouting and threats from her parents and Mayor Ghastly (unfair, I know, three against two, but adults often are unfair) they decided upon a very fitting punishment.

"Seeing as you were both so eager to have slaves for the week," Mrs Darkly began — she had a look on her face that Deirdre could only describe as the look a sabre-toothed tiger might give a blind, one-legged caveman before it pounced — "I think it's only fitting that you both become slaves. Don't you agree, your Honour?"

"Oh yes indeed," agreed the Mayor, stuffing his face with his fifth piece of toast and ever-greater slatherings of Muttonchop's Maggot Marmalade. "Capital idea Mrs Darkly."

"What?" said Spectra and Deirdre together.

"That's right," Mr Darkly continued, "there's more than enough work to be done around here, especially as we're coming up to the summer holidays. It's our busiest time of year and we can always do with an extra pair of hands."

"You mean you want us to work here," said Spectra with a look of utmost disgust plastered across her face. "For a week?" It was as if she had just been asked to clean out the toilets at the Hospital for Extra-Large Elephants with Explosive Diarrhoea.

"Oh no," said the Mayor, "not for a week." Spectra and Deirdre both relaxed a little. "For all six weeks!"

"WHAT!!?" Deirdre and Spectra shrieked at the same time. Spectra shrieked so loudly she almost cracked the glass in both Grandma Hortense's and Grandpa Horace's spectacles — and that was no mean feat; that glass could withstand a charging rhinoceros on roller-skates wearing a crash-helmet.

"I think that's about enough time for you to appreciate the seriousness of your actions," said Mrs Darkly.

"BUT—" they shrieked together again.

"And if you'd like to argue," said Mr Darkly, "we can always give you weekend jobs after the holidays. If you'd like?"

"Now I wish I was the one falling headfirst into the sea…" Deirdre muttered under her breath.

Both she and Spectra knew when they were beaten. They had a common enemy now, not each other but their parents. The Darklys and Mayor Ghastly spent the rest of the morning devising a rota of duties that would make these summer holidays the very worst of their children's lives. Deirdre spent the rest of the day out of sight, in case her parents decided to start her punishment early. On Monday morning she had never been so eager to get to school.

CHAPTER 10
PARPINGTON'S PUZZLING PRONOUNCEMENT

The last day of term arrived and Deirdre's entire class was electric with excitement. During that last week, every teacher in the school had well and truly given up trying to teach their pupils anything. Instead, they had been allowed to play games, bring in toys, read all day or just talk to each other. But not so Mrs Cowl's class. She insisted on making them learn right the way up to the very last second of the last day of term. This might have bothered Deirdre normally, but when she thought about what awaited her at home come the start of the holidays, she didn't mind so much.

She was just copying down the last sum from the blackboard when a small screwed-up piece of paper landed on her desk. She looked to her left and saw Jenny Froggett grinning. Deirdre unscrewed the paper and saw a quickly scrawled note in Jenny's handwriting.

Want to come and have a sleepover at mine in the holidays...?

Deirdre turned the note over, scribbled her reply and threw it back:

I can't, sorry, Mum and Dad have got me working at home ALL SUMMER!!!

Jenny ripped a fresh scrap of paper from her exercise

book and scribbled a new note.

ALL SUMMER!!!! What did you do...???

Deirdre replied:

LOOOOONG story.... Can't wait to leave here. When we do I hope they close the school down!

And then knock it down!

With old Scowly inside!

And Millicent Parpington!

Fighting for the exits!

Through a pack of wild wildebeest!

At Deirdre's last note Jenny gave a rather loud snort of laughter. The entire class turned to look at her, including Mrs Cowl.

"Care to share the joke, Miss Froggett?"

Jenny was about to reply when a rotten little boy with blond hair and a big nose called Jake Snart (the boy was called Jake Snart, not just his nose) threw his hand in the air.

"Please Mrs Cowl," he bleated like a cowardly sheep, "they have been passing notes to each other Mrs Cowl. I've seen them Mrs Cowl!"

110

Deirdre and Jenny looked at Jake Snart with a look of purest hatred. If looks could have killed, Jake Snart would have been worm-food on the spot. But before Mrs Cowl could say anything, another hand had shot into the air and a voice said, "Please Mrs Cowl, they have been passing notes Mrs Cowl. I've seen them too, Mrs Cowl!"

There and then Deirdre Darkly and Jenny Froggett swore an unspoken oath that they would hate Millicent Parpington forever and for always until the end of time. And Jake Snart. But mostly Millicent Parpington.

"How did you see us?" asked Deirdre angrily. "You've got your back to us and you haven't turned around all lesson!"

"So you have been passing notes, have you?" said Mrs Cowl with a wicked smirk.

"Well yes," said Deirdre, "but that's not the point, how could Mil-"

"Don't you tell me what the point is, young lady!" Mrs Cowl's voice had risen to just below 'Danger Level'. The whole class knew it when it got like this. You could either run and hide, or stay and fight. If you ran, no-one in the class thought any worse of you. If you stood and fought, there was no way you could win and, what's more, you stood alone. Deirdre made her choice.

"But how did Millicent see us, Mrs Cowl? She's lying."

"I am not lying, Mrs Cowl, my daddy says that lying is naughty and I'm not a naughty girl, I'm a good little girl, aren't I Mrs Cowl?"

Mrs Cowl smiled a sickening, simpering smile at Millicent Parpington which Millicent returned with gusto. Mrs Cowl turned to Deirdre with a venomous glint in her tiny grey eyes. "Millicent Parpington," she said slowly, "is the very model of good behaviour and honesty and if she says you were passing notes-"

"I saw them too, Mrs Cowl," piped up Jake Snart.

"Shut up, Jake!" Mrs Cowl, Deirdre and Jenny all shouted at once.

"You, Deirdre Darkly, will serve detention, with me tonight. One hour!" The class gasped as one being. Mrs Cowl usually gave out twenty-minute detentions, apart from the half-hour detention she had given to Darren Oakley at the beginning of the year when he'd left a half-starved frog in her desk drawer. When she opened the drawer, it had leapt down her top in an attempt to escape. Mrs Cowl had then done a very surreal version of the Can-Can as she tried to shake it loose. Darren Oakley was expelled soon after and to this day the children still debate which was the more traumatised — teacher or frog.

"But Mrs Cowl," Deirdre began. This was all getting out of hand. Passing a few notes in class just did not merit an hour's detention.

"But nothing!" Mrs Cowl shrieked back. "Do you wish to make it two hours?" The silence was unbearable. The entire class was rapt with awe at the stand-off unfolding before them. Deirdre had chosen to fight in Round One. This was Round Two and every person in that classroom was thinking the same thing. Fight or hide?

"No, Mrs Cowl," said Deirdre, after what felt like an eternity.

"Good!" Mrs Cowl bellowed, "I shall be sending a letter home to your parents this evening. Now, perhaps we could get back to our lesson?"

Deirdre spent the rest of the lesson thinking up horrible revenges on Mrs Cowl and Millicent Parpington. Some of them involved Jake Snart too, but the main tortures were saved especially for her teacher and her worst enemy. She imagined them covered in barbecue sauce and falling spectacularly over a waterfall into crocodile-infested waters. Or being chased by a rabid rhinoceros down a one-way alley. Or falling into a giant wasps' nest whilst covered in strawberry jam.

When lunchtime came, Deirdre was glad of the excuse to leave and hurried out of the classroom as fast as she could. She and Jenny queued up for their dinner, then sat down at a table near the back of the dining hall facing the entrance. They ate in silence for a time, neither of them needing to mention earlier events and choosing instead to watch the activity of the lunch hall. It wasn't long before Millicent Parpington came waltzing in, followed, as usual, by her gang of giggling hyenas. They got their food and sat down in the middle of the hall to eat, laughing uproariously at regular intervals and constantly looking around to see if anybody was watching them.

"I *hate* Millicent Parpington," said Jenny when they had eaten. Millicent got up and made her way to the lunch queue for a dessert, her faithful followers trailing after her like a shoal of Taiwanese Zippy Fish in

July (which is when they are at their most faithful).

Even at the sight of her, Deirdre's insides felt like molten lava when she thought about the detention after school and how it was all Millicent's fault. She began to feel a familiar and frightening prickling sensation underneath her skin, slowly at first then growing.

Jenny got up from her seat, "Are you coming for a dessert?"

Deirdre shook her head, "No thanks. You go, I'm fine."

Jenny smiled and walked off. Deirdre watched Millicent Parpington talking animatedly to one of the dinnerladies, who looked at her the way all the others did — as though she was the most darling thing in the entire world. What Deirdre wouldn't give to see her get her come-uppance. Just a little something. Nothing too horrible, just horrible enough to bring her down a peg or two.

Millicent skipped back across the hall carrying a huge bowl full of trifle. She must have been given three times as much as anyone else because it was almost spilling over the sides. So that was why she was being so nice to the dinnerladies. She looked over in Deirdre's direction and Deirdre felt her temperature rise. The molten lava inside her belly bubbled, ready to erupt, and the white hot needles under her skin felt ready to break through. Her feet and hands began to curl and her shoulder blades started aching. She knew she had to calm herself down — if she wasn't careful her Camouflage might slip again and this time there were far more people around.

Millicent saw that Deirdre was looking at her

and gave her a horrid, mocking, smile then raised a chubby hand and waved. She changed direction and walked towards her. It took all Deirdre's composure not to throw her dinner tray, knife, fork and plate one after the other at Millicent Parpington's big, stupid head and wipe that smile off her face with the remains of her sausages and gravy-soaked cauliflower.

"Hello Eerie Deirdre," she said. Deirdre clenched her fists underneath the table and was horrified when she felt claws digging into her palms instead of nails.

"What do you want, Parpington?" said Deirdre, trying her hardest to keep her voice level.

"Do you like school dinners, Eerie Deirdre?" said Millicent casually.

"Well of course I don't," Deirdre snapped back, "no-one does. Why are you asking me stupid questions, shouldn't you get back to your troop of monkeys? They might get confused if you're not there to show them how to use spoons."

Millicent Parpington simply smiled her sickly-sweet smile. "What kind of food does your hotel serve, Eerie Deirdre…?"

"The finest in Grimley-by-the-Sea, actually," said Deirdre truthfully. "Our Head Chef is French and one of the greatest chefs in the world."

"Hmph!" snorted Millicent. "We'll see…" And on that mysterious note she turned and walked away.

Even after she had left, Deirdre felt the lava bubbling away inside her. Perfect Millicent Parpington thinking she was better than everybody else. What made her so special. Deirdre contemplated dropping her Camouflage and simply swooping down on Millicent, picking her up in her talons, carrying her out over the sea and dropping her straight in it. Then going back for Spectra Ghastly. Then Mrs Cowl. And then perhaps, if there was time, Jake Snart. Even at the thought of her, the red-hot needles underneath Deirdre's skin, the aches in her shoulder-blades and the buzzing in her hands and feet reached a mighty crescendo. She breathed deeply to calm herself down and waited for those all-too-familiar feelings to subside. But they didn't. A flash of terror streaked through Deirdre. The feelings weren't going away. It was almost as if they were out of her control and she was going to drop her Camouflage then and there. There was nothing else for it. Leaving her dinner tray where it was and bumping into a very bemused Jenny Froggett on the way, Deirdre ran out of the dining hall as fast as she could.

She hurtled down the corridor and out into the almost empty playground. Only the fastest packed-lunch eaters were out so early, but Deirdre knew she couldn't risk being spotted by anyone. She ran around the back of the main school building. Normally this was out of bounds to pupils, but this was an emergency. Though the excuse, 'sorry, Sir, but I'm secretly a gargoyle, I felt like I was about to transform and wanted a bit of privacy' probably wouldn't be taken seriously enough. Not by the teaching staff of Gravely Down Junior School at any rate. Deirdre sat down with her back to the wall as she tried desperately to calm herself. After several minutes she began to feel the prickling, bubbling sensations fade and her heartbeat slow to its normal rhythm.

"That was too close," she muttered to herself. "I'll be glad when I'm out of this place."

She had just got to her feet and was about to walk back around to the playground when she found herself once again diving out of sight. Straight ahead was her classroom, which overlooked the spare scrap of land she was hiding in. The classroom should have been deserted, but Deirdre had seen something — or someone — move. Her natural curiosity overcame her fear of being caught in forbidden territory as she crept forwards to get a better look. Peering ever-so-slightly over the top of the windowsill, she saw Mrs Cowl sitting at her desk and eating her lunch; she had her back to Deirdre. Deirdre thought it was strange that she wasn't in the staff room.

Peeping around Mrs Cowl's bony frame, Deirdre saw a small, plastic box on her desk that had no doubt contained her lunch. It was empty apart from one last item, a small, red thing about the size of an apple covered in brown, wriggling things. It was the wriggling that caught Deirdre's attention. Before she could look any closer, Mrs Cowl had reached across and grabbed the mystery object in her talon-like fingers. Deirdre nearly fell over backwards as it came clearly into view. It was a heart. A cow's heart covered in live maggots. Mrs Cowl took a huge bite before wiping the blood off her chin with a napkin. Deirdre gasped. As a monster she was used to seeing sights like this, especially living in a hotel. But from her teacher? Her *Typical* teacher?

She must have gasped louder than she thought

because, at that moment, Mrs Cowl turned around. Moving faster than she ever thought she could, Deirdre threw herself against the wall praying that the small ledge underneath the window might go some way to hiding her. She waited for what felt like a lifetime before finally sneaking away, terrified that at any moment she would be halted by the rapping of Mrs Cowl's knuckles on the classroom window.

Deirdre spent the rest of lunchtime in a daze. Questions tumbled through her brain like Wilhelmina down a flight of stairs. She was dying to tell Jenny what she had seen, but knew that if she did she might accidentally let something slip about her and her real monstrous identity.

Back in the classroom, Deirdre couldn't stop thinking about what she had just seen. She had been over and over it constantly for the remainder of dinner, and she still couldn't think of a reasonable explanation. A cow's heart covered in maggots was something of a refreshing snack in Grimley-by-the-Sea. Monsieur Volcan could whip up a delicious batch in minutes. So what was her Typical teacher doing munching merrily away on such fine monstrous cuisine at dinnertime? When Mrs Cowl stalked into the classroom, Deirdre kept her head down. She didn't need to get into any more trouble today.

"Good afternoon class," said Mrs Cowl.

"Good afternoooooon Mrs Cooooowuuullllll," the class chanted back.

"Before I take the register," Mrs Cowl continued, "I have a little end of term treat for you all." She produced a large cardboard box from underneath her

desk and opened it. "There's one for each of you," —
Deirdre felt her heart begin to race once more —
"They're a particular delicacy where I come from."
Deirdre felt like she was going to be sick — gifts were
not Mrs Cowl's speciality. "I couldn't wait, I'm afraid
and had one myself at dinnertime…" What was going
on? Mrs Cowl reached inside the box and Deirdre felt
the panic and fear well up inside her. With a flourish
Mrs Cowl produced a small, round thing on a stick that
was about the size of an apple. Deirdre looked away,
waiting to hear the gasps and screams of horror — but
they didn't come. Gasps and cheers of delight filled the
room instead.

"Toffee apples!" Mrs Cowl declared
triumphantly. "I've one for each of you." She began
moving between the desks, handing them out to her
delighted (not to mention flabbergasted) pupils.
Deirdre felt more than a little bit stupid. Toffee apples.
That was what she had seen Mrs Cowl eating at lunch.

"Where did you get them from, Miss?" asked a
boy named Brian Corduroy.

"There's a little shop on the high street of the
village I live in," said Mrs Cowl. "They make them
using an ancient family recipe." She continued to hand
out the apples. "They can even come with little toffee
sprinkles on top. They're my favourite kind."

Deirdre nearly fainted with relief. A toffee apple
with little toffee sprinkles on top. How could she have
been so silly? All that worry and panic over her lunch
break. She almost laughed out loud she felt so relieved.
Mrs Cowl came to a stop by her desk. She reached
inside the box and then stopped. A rather over-the-top

confused expression appeared on her wrinkled old face. Deirdre could hear those claw-like fingernails scratching around at the bottom of the box.

"Oh my, would you look at that," said Mrs Cowl. "It seems they got my order wrong and delivered one too few. Oh well, never mind." She peered at Deirdre over her half-moon spectacles for a few moments before striding back to her desk.

"Here," whispered Jenny when Mrs Cowl was far enough away, "have this one."

"No need, Miss Froggett," barked Mrs Cowl without turning around. "Judging from her expression as she watched me eating mine this lunchtime, I doubt they would be to her liking. Am I correct, Miss Darkly?"

Deirdre said nothing.

CHAPTER 11
AN UNEXPECTED INSPECTION

All in all the last afternoon of term was, perhaps, one of Deirdre's worst ever. She didn't get to talk with Jenny, or read any books or even play 'hangman' on the blackboard. What's more, it lasted a whole hour longer than it should have done. She trudged out of Gravely Down Junior School at half-past four and got into the old horse-drawn carriage where Mr Prendergast was waiting. As the carriage trundled off, she didn't even give the place one final look. Mrs Cowl had kept her there to the last second and enjoyed every moment of her final punishment. Deirdre's sole consolation was that she had seen the last of Mrs Cowl and Millicent Parpington *forever*.

The carriage ride home seemed to take no time at all — as is usual when you are heading toward something you are dreading. A trip to the dentist, for example, or a visit from an old aunt who insists on kissing you and pinching your cheeks whenever she comes within five feet. The time seems to fly by at triple speed and, before you know it, it's here.

Spectra was already waiting in reception when Deirdre got home. She was dressed in scruffy overalls and what was unmistakeably one of Uncle Dilbert's old and overly large bandanas on her head. Deirdre would have laughed at the sight had she not felt so rotten.

"Ah, there you are Deirdre," said her mother. "You're late!"

"Detention," Deirdre mumbled. There wasn't much point pretending otherwise; it wasn't like her parents could punish her any more than they were doing.

"Really?" Mrs Darkly raised her eyebrows. "Well, what a way to end your school career at Gravely Down Junior School. Spectra's been waiting for you; we didn't think it was right that she start without you. There are some overalls for you behind reception; once you're dressed you can both start on the first-floor toilets. They need cleaning rather urgently, if you know what I mean?"

"Why?" asked Deirdre, though she suspected she didn't really want to know the answer.

Mrs Darkly lowered her voice. "We think Monsieur Volcan may have undercooked the roast kraken last night and it's given some of our guests... well... you'll need these —" she threw each of them a large pair of bright yellow rubber gloves, "and these —" she threw two pairs of old mismatched Wellington boots. "Good luck!" Mrs Darkly trilled as she left them alone staring at the gloves and Wellingtons and feeling very sorry for themselves.

And so the weeks rolled by. To Deirdre, they passed in a blur of scrubbed floors, swept carpets, cobwebbed corners, dusted mantelpieces, mopped kitchens, washing-up, cooking and general non-stop work. She and Spectra hardly spoke to each other the whole time, each blaming the other for their sorry fate. They were most often in the same room together either polishing the suits of armour, or making sure the portraits of past Darklys were all straight where they hung. Despite this, they were resigned not to make things worse by talking to each other. But all that was about to change, as exactly three weeks into the summer holidays a most unexpected guest arrived at the Darkly Manor Hotel.

The hotel was as busy as it had ever been. Almost every room was full and Mr and Mrs Darkly were run off their feet, — which meant that they spent less time harassing their unfortunate 'slaves'. This, of course, gave Spectra and Deirdre more opportunity to relax a little with their chores, as Deirdre's parents were often far too busy to keep checking in on them. It was one Monday morning just after breakfast when things took a very serious turn for the worse. Deirdre was behind the reception desk, crouched low while trying to prise a particularly stubborn blob of Wiggly's Fearmint chewing gum from out of the carpet. Her parents were also behind reception, busily jotting things down in the guest-book, scribbling things down on order forms and generally fussing like grown-ups do. In the middle of her battle with the chewing gum, Deirdre heard footsteps approaching the desk. A rather brash voice announced —

"My name is Alastair Parpington and I would like a room."

At the name 'Parpington' Deirdre nearly leapt out of her skin. *Parpington*? But it *couldn't* be. Could it? She crept closer to a small crack in the large wooden desk and peered through. The man was standing some way back, looking around the entrance hall. He was tall, thin, had a neatly trimmed moustache and neat, black hair slicked back in an oily centre-parting. He wore bright white trousers, a crisp, white shirt, a cricket jumper tied around his shoulders and wicker slip-on shoes on his feet. He was fanning himself with a white panama hat in his left hand and a light, canary-coloured jacket was slung over his right arm.

"Certainly sir," Mr Darkly looked up and smiled at the man. "Will your daughter be staying with you, or would you like two rooms?"

Alastair Parpington sniffed haughtily and then sighed, "I have already asked you for *a* room, have I not? To my mind that speaks of *one* room. I do *not* like repeating myself, pray do not make me do so again." Mr Darkly said nothing but Mrs Darkly had now looked up from her work. Deirdre could see she was looking at Parpington as though she would like nothing better than to ram his panama hat down his throat. "And Millicent is *not* my daughter; she is my niece and she will be sharing a room with me."

Deirdre felt her entire body go cold. She knew she had heard it, but in her head she was busy telling herself she had *mis*heard it. She started going through all the other Millicent Parpingtons there might be in the world, convincing herself that it was an extremely common name. Lots of girls are called Millicent Parpington. Hundreds of them. Maybe even thousands. But it was no use. She knew, deep down, that there was only *one* Millicent Parpington and she was here, right at that very moment, in Deirdre's home.

Almost immediately another, even more terrifying, thought ran through her head. Millicent Parpington and her Uncle Alastair were *Typicals*. They had no business being in Grimley-by-the-Sea at all. She had to warn her parents. Looking up at them, her heart pounding inside her chest fit to burst, she saw that they had both, by extraordinary coincidence, adopted their Camouflaged forms. She supposed the lack of screams from Millicent and her uncle when they had entered the room should have told her something was not quite right. She silently thanked the past few weeks for being so busy that her mother and father's stress levels had Camouflaged them automatically.

"We'll get you and your lovely niece a room right away, Mr Parpington," she heard her mother say in the sickly-sweet manner she always adopted for incredibly rude people.

Deirdre tugged on her father's trouser leg and whispered, *"Dad!"*, but Mr Darkly was busy rifling through the vast log-book of rooms checking for one that was available. "Dad!" Deirdre whispered a little louder this time and tugged a little harder, but still Mr Darkly ignored her and kept on rifling. *"DAD!"* With one final tug Mr Darkly came tumbling down behind reception to land in a heap next to his daughter.

"Deirdre!" he whispered in outright shock. "What on earth do you think you're doing?"

"Dad, you have to listen to me," Deirdre gasped. "That girl, she goes to my school, or at least she *did* go, I mean, go to my *old* school, I mean we've both left *now*, but —"

"Deirdre," Mr Darkly interrupted in a serious tone, "I don't have time for this nonsense, now let me up."

He made to get to his feet but Deirdre grabbed the front of his tank-top, pulled his face close to hers and whispered through gritted teeth. "They're Typicals!"

The colour drained from Mr Darkly's face and for one terrifying moment Deirdre thought her father's Camouflage had slipped and he was back in his natural vampire form. "B-b-but…" he stammered, "h-h-how… w-w-why…?"

"There's no time for questions, Dad, we need to get them out of here right this minute! It's a miracle they made it this far without seeing anyone! Or without being eaten!"

"Right," said Mr Darkly steadying himself. He stood to his feet in one fluid motion and said, "I'm terribly sorry about that, Mr Parpington, but it appears we have no rooms available at present."

Deirdre could see her mother looking at him with a bemused expression on her face. This, in itself, was nothing unusual.

"Yes we do," she said, shuffling through the guest-book herself. "We may be busy but I think we can find one room for Mr Parpington and his niece. Look," she pointed to a vacant space in the book, "Room 513, that's free."

"No it's not," said Mr Darkly quickly, "sorry dear, I forgot to write it down, but a family of ghouls… I mean… a family… the *Goulds*, yes — a family, the Goulds, arrived this morning and I put them in Room 513."

"Well then," Mrs Darkly re-checked the log-book, "Room 609's free, we can put Mr Parpington in there."

"No we can't," said Mr Darkly, "a couple of young spooks… a spook… spook-tacular… a *spectacular* young couple from Argentina are in there. On their honeymoon, don't you know… Ha ha, young love and all that, wouldn't want to disturb them, would we?"

"Well," said Mrs Darkly, getting more confused *and* annoyed with her husband by the second, "Room 696 then!"

"Trolls," Mr Darkly bellowed, "I mean… *trawl…s…* trawl through that whole book and you won't find a free room in this entire hotel!"

"We've found three so far," said Parpington haughtily. "I must say I think you're both *extremely* unprofessional *and* inefficient." He took out a blue notepad and pencil and began scribbling something down.

"Well *really*," Mrs Darkly began and Deirdre knew what was coming. Mr Parpington was about to get a good ear-bashing, or perhaps — even worse — he could have his nose turned into a ferret, or his hair turned into millipedes.

Deirdre knew the time was right for action. Throwing caution aside (as well as her pride as she remembered too late just what she was wearing and how she must look) she donned her Camouflage and leapt to her feet.

"Hello Millicent!" she shrieked in the most over-the-top cheerful voice she could muster. "How *are* you? Enjoying the *school* holidays?" She hoped the emphasis on the word 'school' might do the trick and let her mother know just what a state they were in.

It didn't exactly work. It did, however, do the job of making Millicent and her uncle both jump out of their skin, so all was not wasted. Millicent recovered her usual snide composure almost immediately.

"Hello Deirdre," she simpered, "I thought I'd see you here." Seeing as this was Deirdre's home, that wasn't an *incredibly* clever prediction to make, but this was neither the time nor the place to point that out. Millicent looked Deirdre up and down in her scruffy, ill-fitting overalls and overly large bandana. She broke into such a smile it was if all her birthdays had come at once and she had just adopted an entire herd of new ponies. "What*ever* are you wearing?"

"Mum?" said Deirdre turning to her mother. "*This* is Millicent Parpington, we know each other from *school*, Mum, we go to the same *school*, Millicent and me."

"Millicent and *I*," said Parpington interrupting. "I must say your child's grammar is as poor as the service in this hotel. Tell me, have you ever *heard* of organisation?" Mrs Darkly had now gone as pale as her husband and had started shooting surreptitious glances around the entrance hall. "*I*," Parpington continued, "am a representative from the International League of Hotel Inspectors." He drew out a large, highly polished gold badge from his pocket that shone brightly in the dim entrance hall. "And I am here for an inspection of your premises." The Darklys went silent. This could *not* be happening. "We at the ILHI have no records whatsoever about this hotel. In fact, it's almost as if it doesn't exist outside of this… *quaint* little village, which, I confess, I had never even heard of until recently. I intend to stay for one week, at the end of which I shall give you your marks after sampling everything this hotel has to offer."

It was Mr Darkly who found his voice first.

"H... How did you find out about us?"

"Ah," said Parpington, turning to his niece and giving her the same sickening smile Deirdre had seen every grown-up that ever went near her give, "you have my darling Millicent to thank for that. She told me that her good friend Deirdre here lived in a hotel and that it was in dire need of an inspection. Didn't you dear?"

"Uncle Alastair is soooo important, Deirdre," Millicent was doing a terrible job of hiding her sheer delight at the trouble she had caused, "he can make or break a hotel's reputation just like that," she clicked her fingers. "He can even close *really* bad hotels down... forever..."

"No!" Deirdre couldn't stop herself, this was all too much.

"Oh yes, little girl," Parpington grinned. "I have it in my authority to do whatever is necessary to make sure this hotel is up to my... *exacting* standards... Now, about that room..."

"Why yes," said Mrs Darkly after a few moments, "step right this way, won't you, and I'll show you both to your room at once."

"Well it's about time," said Parpington, rocking back on his heels. "Now you," he gestured flippantly with one hand to Mr Darkly, "go and get our bags from outside." Mr Darkly jumped as though he had just been given an electric shock. He practically ran out of the door to the Parpington's car.

"Won't you follow me, Mr Parpington? Miss Parpington?" said Mrs Darkly. "I'll show you to your room while my husband follows with your bags?"

"Very well," said Parpington. "Millicent dear, go and call for the lift, there's a good girl."

"NO!" Deirdre and Mrs Darkly shrieked together as in their minds they both formed an image. What a treat, the lift doors sliding open to reveal Graham the giant ape looming out at them with his too-small bright red jacket and tiny bellboy's hat perched on his giant monkey-head.

"Why don't we take the stairs?" said Mrs Darkly, "the lift is out of... I mean the lift is not... Why don't we take the stairs?"

"To the sixth floor?" said Parpington in disbelief.

"Exercise!" said Deirdre. thinking faster than she had ever done in her life. "We... er... always try and encourage exercise at the Darkly Manor Hotel."

"That's right!" Mrs Darkly agreed. "Exercise! Off we go!" She began jogging vigorously and rather ridiculously on the spot before grabbing the key for Room 696. She sidled out of reception and ushered Millicent and her uncle up the stairs.

Mr Darkly appeared seconds later out of breath, his arms full of suitcases. "Where have they gone?" he gasped.

"Mum's showing them to their room," said Deirdre. "Dad, what are we going to do?"

"I don't know," said Mr Darkly, dropping two suitcases. "Why didn't your mother let me get rid of them? I tried to tell them we haven't got any rooms free."

Deirdre shrugged, "I suppose she thought two Typicals inside a hotel full of Fright Folk isn't as bad as two Typicals outside in an entire *village* full of Fright

130

Folk. I mean, it's a miracle they didn't see anyone or anything suspicious on their journey here, isn't it?"

"I suppose so," Mr Darkly agreed, "and speaking of miracles, we're going to need one to get out of this in one piece."

Deirdre didn't say anything. She just let the words of Millicent Parpington float through her brain... *"He can even close really bad hotels down... forever "*

CHAPTER 12
THE GRAND TOUR

Mr Darkly rushed the Parpingtons' luggage up the stairs and returned several minutes later with Mrs Darkly. Both of them looked as though they were about to be sick.

"What are we going to do?" Deirdre asked her mother this time.

"I'm not sure," said Mrs Darkly. "How could this have happened?"

"I don't know," said Mr Darkly as though these three words were the only ones any of them could utter. "How did anyone outside Grimley find out about us?"

"*Millicent*," said Deirdre, oozing venom with every syllable, "that's who. She's always hated me and now she's trying to shut down my home."

Mr Darkly had begun to pace and was pulling out tufts of his already thinning hair. "How on earth are we going to keep a hotel full of Fright Folk all hidden until they leave?"

"We can't," said Mrs Darkly. "It's as simple as that. We're too full. The summer holidays are our busiest time of year."

"There must be *something* we can do," said Deirdre. "If they find out what we are, then we'll have bigger problems than the hotel closing down."

"Deirdre's right," said Mr Darkly, "there'll be photographers and newspapers and monster-hunters and scientists wanting to do experiments on us and —"

"Alright," said Mrs Darkly, "I know what we

have to do. We have to somehow let everyone in the hotel know about the Typicals."

"How are we going to do that?" asked Deirdre. "The hotel is *full*!"

"I don't know *how*, exactly," said Mrs Darkly, "but there *has* to be a way through this."

"But—" Deirdre began but her father spoke over her.

"But nothing, Deirdre, we've no other choice. They're here now and they're staying! We'll just have to take one day at a time. It might not be so bad. Everyone can wear their Camouflage."

"But Dad," said Deirdre, "what about those *without* Camouflage, and what about Kevin, and the talking rats in the basement, and the gardens and *Barry*?"

At this the stuffed zombie moose head behind Reception stirred in his sleep and opened one droopy eyelid. "Someone call...?" he muttered sleepily.

"GO TO SLEEP, BARRY!" the three Darklys barked as one.

"Right-ho," said Barry, who promptly fell straight back to sleep again.

"You see?" said Mr Darkly positively. "We probably won't even have to worry about Barry at all!"

Just then, Spectra walked in through the dining-room doors, her banshee hair dishevelled and decidedly dirtier for all her hard work. She had been mopping the trophy-room floor while Deirdre had been on chewing-gum duty. "I need more water," she said holding up her empty mop bucket.

"Spectra!" the Darklys once again spoke

together, only this time in a shouted whisper.

"Put your Camouflage on!" said Deirdre.

"What?" said Spectra looking puzzled. "Why?"

"Because there are Typicals in the hotel," answered Deirdre, "and they can't—"

"WHAT?" Spectra shrieked. "Typicals! HERE?"

"YES!" Deirdre whispered, running over to her and clamping a hand over her mouth.

"But that's impossible," said Spectra, "Typicals don't exist in Grimley except in nightmares!"

"Well," said Mrs Darkly, "it looks like our nightmares are coming true." She ran around the reception desk and scribbled a short note on a scrap of paper, laid the paper on the table and then waved her hand over it several times while muttering to herself. The one piece of paper instantly multiplied into a great teetering stack of papers, which Mrs Darkly split into two piles handing one each to Deirdre and Spectra. "Take these and post them under every door to every room, okay girls?"

Deirdre looked at the note. It read:

ATTENTION HOTEL GUESTS

It is with great regret that we must inform you that this hotel is currently being occupied by two Typicals, a hotel inspector and his young niece. It is our wish that we avoid any unpleasantness and, to that end, we would like to invite you all to a meeting tonight at *midnight in the lounge to discuss our options. In the meantime please take every care not to be seen out without Camouflage.*

Thank you in advance,

Mrs D. Darkly,
Co-Proprietor.

"What are you and Dad going to do?" asked Deirdre, looking up from her stack of notes.

"Well…" Mrs Darkly thought for a few moments, "Dexter, you go and see which guests are not in their rooms. Check the grounds, the games room, the swimming pool… Oh, try and find your Mum, Dad and Bert and let them know what's going on."

"Right," said Mr Darkly, "but what about you? What will you do?"

"I'll go and wait outside their door in case they leave. Here, give me some of those," she took a stack of papers from Deirdre's pile, "I'll do the sixth floor, you two start from the fifth floor and work your way down." Deirdre nodded and ran off up the stairs followed by a grumpy Spectra.

"How on *earth* are we going to deliver all of these?" Spectra wafted her substantial pile of notes beneath Deirdre's nose.

"By not wasting time moaning and complaining about it," Deirdre snapped back. The time they had spent together had so far done nothing to diminish their mutual loathing.

"But it'll take ages," Spectra groaned, "and they could catch us at any minute!"

Deirdre hated to admit it, but Spectra was right. Delivering all the notes by hand would take an awfully long time and it was important that they all got delivered fast.

"You know," droned Spectra, "when my father hears about this, he'll have something to say about it."

"What do you think he'll do?" asked Deirdre. "Scare them off or something?"

"Well…" said Spectra, "no, but he'll… well he'll…"

"Exactly," said Deirdre, "this is unheard of in the entire history of Grimley-by-the-Sea: there *are* no procedures. And besides, it's the law that we have to remain hidden when there are Typicals around. You know that and I'm sure your Dad knows that."

"Well of course he does," Spectra snapped.

"Good," said Deirdre, "now can we please just get on with this?"

"Fine, but if you think I'm coming back here tomorrow with two Typicals hanging around the place then you're wrong!"

"Fine!" Deirdre snapped back. "It won't make any difference anyway the amount of work you do! Now wait here."

They had reached a floor with a wide landing and no rooms on it. There was just the one door, a shabby green thing with peeling paint and a 'No Entry' sign on it. Deirdre checked to see if the coast was clear then dropped her Camouflage, opened the door and snuck inside.

136

"Where are you going?" Spectra hissed. She thought several times about following Deirdre, but kept losing her nerve. It wasn't long before Deirdre returned, breathless and looking rather pleased with herself. "Where have you been?" growled Spectra.

"Belfry," said Deirdre, gesturing toward the peeling green door. "Why, did you miss me? Scared the big, bad Typicals were going to get you…?"

"Don't be stupid," said Spectra, going slightly red. "What were you doing up there anyway?"

"Gathering the troops," Deirdre smiled smugly.

"What?"

"You'll see. Just you wait."

They didn't have to wait long. Within a few seconds there came the faint sound of rustling from behind the green door. It was steadily getting louder and louder. Deirdre stepped forward and opened the door just in time for what seemed like hundreds of little black bats to come pouring out. They circled for a few seconds before coming to a stop, landing in several perfectly straight rows. One bat still fluttered above them. It landed a few moments later in front of Deirdre and Spectra. This bat was slightly larger than the rest and looked different — mainly because of the green General's cap on its head, the row of tiny medals on its chest and the pipe sticking out of its mouth. A few bubbles spilled over the sides of the pipe as the bat spoke.

"All present and correct, ma'am! Awaiting your instructions, ma'am!"

Deirdre smiled as Spectra looked on with her mouth open as wide as a starving wide-mouthed frog amidst a plague of blind bluebottles.

The head bat turned to Spectra and announced, "Don't believe I've had the pleasure, ma'am. Field Marshall Wilberforce Fothergill-Pennington-Smythe, at your service. Call me Wilber if it's easier."

"Her name's Spectra," said Deirdre, as Spectra was still doing her incredibly realistic wide-mouthed frog impersonation. "I wouldn't bother remembering it, she won't be with us long."

"Ah, Stinking Grot-Marsh Fever, eh?" said Field Marshall Wilberforce Fothergill-Penn — said Wilber. "Knew a chap caught that back in East Africa in '64. Drove him mad before it took him. Spent the last few days of his life thinking he was a garden rake."

"No," said Deirdre, "she's not got Stinking Grot-Marsh Fever."

"The Withering Snap, then? Have your palms turned green?"

"She's not got that either!"

"The Shrieking Vapours? Frog-spit Fever? The Spiralling Gout?"

"She's not ill at all, Field Marshall," said Deirdre, losing her patience. "Look, we need your help and we need it urgently."

Deirdre told Field Marshall Wilber and his troops — the Bat Battalion — what was happening in the hotel, of the imminent danger and the need for stealth at all times.

"You can count on us, ma'am, don't you worry," said Wilber, turning to face his troops. "Right lads, hear this now. We've got a job to do and we're *damn* sure going to do it. And do it right. Now, as you all know

138

some of us might not make it back from this mission. That's mainly because tonight it's the hundred and nineteenth annual Grimley All-Monster Tiddlywinks Championships at eleven. Lord knows we don't want to miss that. Let's wrap this up and wrap it up quickly so we can be there when the Grimley Gargoyles smash the Grimsditch Gorgons with their superior pieces of coloured circular plastic. You know what they say, hundred and nineteenth time lucky. On my orders then… Quick… Fly!"

The bats flew one after the other like a giant black whip being cracked. Each one swooped forward and plucked a note from either Deirdre or Spectra's pile then flapped off and out of sight.

"That reminds me!" shouted Deirdre over the noise. "You don't need to go to the sixth floor, my Mum's seeing to it."

"What's that?" barked Wilber, who happened to be as deaf as a llama with no ears. "There's a fresh batch of snow on the sixth floor and your Mum's weeing through it?"

"No!" shrieked Deirdre, "That's nothing *like* what I said!"

"Don't you worry about your Mummy, little Deirdre!" shouted Wilber taking flight himself now. "We'll soon have her out of that snowdrift. Come on lads, we've got a messy woman to save!"

"No!" Deirdre shouted after them. "Wait!"

"Well that went well," said Spectra, as the bats disappeared on their mission.

"It'll be alright," said Deirdre, trying to convince herself more than Spectra, "they'll see Mum's fine and she'll get rid of them. Come on, we better get back downstairs and help Dad find the others."

As they reached the entrance hall, Mr Darkly came running in from the dining room.

"Everything alright?" he asked breathlessly.

"Fine," said Deirdre, shooting Spectra a glance. "Did you find everyone?"

"I found your grandparents, they were up in their room. I've told them to stay there until we figure out what to do. I couldn't find your Uncle Bert."

"Oh he'll be alright," said Deirdre, though not quite believing herself, "he doesn't even need Camouflage. Where's Mum?"

As if on cue they heard Mrs Darkly speaking much louder than normal as she came down the stairs. "Well of *course* Mr Parpington, a tour of our facilities would be an *excellent* idea...!"

"Look out!" Mr Darkly started jumping up and down on the spot. "They're coming!"

"What do you want us to do, Dad?" said Deirdre. "There's no-one around and we're all Camouflaged!"

Mr Darkly stopped jumping up and down on the spot. "Oh, right, so you are. Well... just... carry on."

Mrs Darkly was first into the entrance hall, her face nervous and her eyes darting in every direction. "But are you *sure* you wouldn't like to rest awhile first? You must have had a long drive...?"

"Millicent is resting," said Parpington, who was carrying a notepad and pen, "*I*, on the other hand, have no time for rest. I should like to get on with this as soon as I am able. Now, shall we begin? Lead on!"

Mrs Darkly threw a wide-eyed glance at Mr Darkly, who guessed at once what it might mean. Fifteen years of marriage was long enough to develop a fairly keen sense of what the other was thinking in extreme circumstances.

"Right you are, Inspector!" said Mr Darkly, practically sprinting ahead of them to the dining-room doors. "Just follow me!" He opened one of the doors just a crack and peered round it. With all the subtlety of a Tyrannosaurus Rex let loose on a Secret Government Farm for Unnaturally Slow Experimental Giant Chickens, Mr Darkly grinned at the others before giving them an enthusiastic double thumbs-up.

Mrs Darkly, Deirdre and Spectra all looked at one another and sighed. "Just coming dear," Mrs Darkly said with much forced cheeriness. "After you, Mr Parpington." As Parpington nodded briskly and strode toward Mr Darkly's grinning visage, Mrs Darkly bent low to Spectra and Deirdre and whispered, "Whose idea was it to get Captain Dingbat and his Idiot Brigade to deliver those notes? I only just managed to get them off the landing in time."

"I thought we could use them to deliver the notes quickly," said Deirdre. "Sorry Mum."

"Never mind that now," said Mrs Darkly, "just be more careful in future. Now go and keep an eye on that niece of his, make sure she doesn't leave her room!"

"Right," said Deirdre, "leave it to us."

"Oh, and Deirdre?" Mrs Darkly called her back. Deirdre and Spectra stopped and turned around. "Why were the bats all sniggering and handing me rolls of loo paper?"

"Must be an army thing," Deirdre said, flushing light pink.

Deirdre and an unwilling Spectra ran back up the stairs to the sixth floor. When they reached Room 696, they crept up to the door and cupped their ears to it. There was the muffled sound of movement coming from inside.

"She's probably unpacking," Deirdre whispered.

"But how are we going to keep her in there?" asked Spectra. "She can't unpack forever!"

Just then, Uncle Dilbert rounded a corner whistling loudly. Deirdre and Spectra both jumped so high their heads nearly hit the ceiling. "Hello girls," he said cheerfully, "heard about the You-Know-Whats we got stayin'?"

"Sshhh!" Spectra and Deirdre both made violent 'shushing' motions with their hands.

"How did you find out?" asked Deirdre. "Dad said he couldn't find you."

Uncle Dilbert sniffed then shrugged, "I was playing cards with a couple of gorgons and a Minotaur in Room 314 when this slip of paper came under the door."

"Well," said Deirdre indicating Room 696, "one of them is in *here*…"

Uncle Dilbert's cheerful smile vanished. "In there, you say…?"

"Yes," said Spectra, "her uncle's taking a tour and we need to make sure we keep *her* in *here*."

Deirdre looked at Spectra with a confused expression. After a few moments she said, "You seem awfully eager to help all of a sudden."

142

"Well," Spectra replied huffily, "the sooner we get today over with the sooner I can get home and be done with all this nonsense." Deirdre rolled her eyes and pulled an 'I thought so' face.

"So…" said Uncle Dilbert, "you need her keeping in there, do you…? I might have just the thing…"

He waggled his stubby fingers and muttered a few words under his breath. Deirdre began to back away from the door as a dread sense of fear welled up inside her. All of a sudden a bright yellow and red ball of fire shot from Uncle Dilbert's hands toward the door of Room 696. Deirdre and Spectra just about had time to leap out of the way before the door blew clean off its hinges and then disintegrated before their very eyes. Millicent screamed and leapt three feet into the air. Her terror did not stem purely from the fact that she now found herself looking through an empty doorframe. Nor was it entirely because the remains of said door (two extremely charred hinges) were at that moment smouldering in a pile of ash by her feet. It was mainly because at that moment she happened to be dressed in only a frilly, pink swimming costume.

"Hello Millicent…" said Deirdre, her voice shaking slightly, "everything alright with the room…?"

143

Captain Blatch stood, as ever, at the head of the trolley on top of a large sponge, his forepaw dramatically shading his black beady eyes, his front leg raised on a bar of soap and his tail swishing to and fro in the breeze.

CHAPTER 13
CAPTAIN BLATCH AND HIS BARMY BAND OF BRAZEN BUCCANEERS... AND BARBARA

Meanwhile, downstairs Mr and Mrs Darkly and Mr Parpington had entered the — thankfully deserted — dining room.

"As you can see," said Mr Darkly, his eyes constantly darting this way and that, "this is the dining room..."

"Obviously," said Parpington, picking up a fork and peering closely at it. "Filthy..." he muttered, seemingly to himself although still loud enough for Mr and Mrs Darkly to hear.

"Oh, that's because the cutlery hasn't been cleaned yet," said Mr Darkly conversationally. As soon as he had said it he turned to Mrs Darkly, whose face mirrored his own. Sheer horror.

"The cutlery hasn't been *cleaned* yet?" said Parpington, incredulously.

"The cutlery hasn't been cleaned yet!" Mr and Mrs Darkly turned to face each other.

Mr Darkly took out his pocket-watch and glanced at it. His eyes widened as he thrust the golden fob watch in his wife's face. "And *look* at the time, dear!"

For those of you who are unfamiliar with the long list of duties performed in the Darkly Manor Hotel on any given day, I shall now attempt to explain. After the breakfast foods have been cleared away and the kitchens are busy preparing for lunch, all the plates and cutlery are cleaned by Captain Blatch and his Band of Brazen Buccaneers. What's so strange or terrifying about *that*, I hear you cry? Well, for one, Captain Blatch is a great, brown rat. Captain Blatch's Band of Brazen Buccaneers are also rats, though not all of them are great or brown. Some are small, some fat, some are long and thin. However, all of them are rats. And if there's one thing a hotel inspector does not like to see on an inspection it's a horde of vermin swarming all over the plates and cutlery. Even if they are an incredibly clean horde of vermin and they do a marvellous job, that still won't change his reaction.

Captain Blatch and his crew were once a very ordinary and in no way rat-like band of pirates. They enjoyed the usual piratey things — cursing, sailing, looting, swashbuckling and saying 'Arrrr' as many times in one sentence as possible. One dark, stormy night (of course), they docked at a strange port for fresh supplies. They decided to stay the night at an old inn called The Creaking Sheep, that was owned by an old hag called Madame Murp. Now Madame Murp owned a shabby, fat black cat she called Mr Wigglesworth whom she loved dearly. To the end of his days Captain Blatch could never *fully* remember the exact sequence of events that led to him and his pirate band being turned into rodents, but he did learn a very valuable lesson that has stayed with him forever. *NEVER* kick a witch's cat out of a top-floor window because it's done a wee on your favourite hat.

It took the men a while to adjust to life as rodents, but they were a resourceful bunch and soon found they were still able to sail a pirate ship well enough. The cursing, sailing, looting and swashbuckling, however, became somewhat trickier. It is rather difficult to be intimidating when you're only six inches tall and have a tail and a twitchy little nose. On the upside, saying 'Arrrr' as many times in one sentence as possible still came very naturally to them.

There are not many jobs available for rats who were once pirates when the piracy dries up. There aren't *that* many jobs where a rat can say 'Arrrr' as many times as it likes. But, as it happened, these once piratical rats still knew how to swab a deck with the best of them. So when they eventually found their way to Grimley-by-the-Sea (as all strange and unfortunate creatures will do), employment in the catering industry beckoned.

Every day after helping chop, stir, sauté, pan-fry, slice, dice and curry in the kitchens, at eleven o'clock on the dot Captain Blatch and his Band of Brazen Buccaneers would all roll into the dining room. Instead of a ship, they now commandeered a large trolley filled with bowls of soapy water, cloths, polish and a mop, and their job was to clean the dining room from top to bottom. What's more, they had never missed a day in three hundred years, nor had they ever been even a second late to perform their duties. Mr Darkly watched helplessly as the second-hand on his pocket-watch ticked unstoppably around the watch-face and the minute-hand ticked inevitably on to the number eleven.

As if on cue, the doors to the utility room next to the kitchen burst open and out rolled a great rattling trolley piled high with cleaning utensils and piled even higher with debonair and charismatic rats. Captain

Blatch stood, as ever, at the head of the trolley on top of a large sponge, his forepaw dramatically shading his black beady eyes, his front leg raised on a bar of soap and his tail swishing to and fro in the breeze. He was still every inch the handsome pirate captain he had been centuries ago. One of his large ears held an even larger gold hoop in it, he wore a decadent purple and gold sash across his little furry chest, a red bandana on his head and a tiny rat-sized eye-patch over his right eye. A small sword made from an old razorblade stuck in a handle made from a cork hung by his side. His crew were not too dissimilar from their captain; some wore hats with feathers in and some had terrible scars or tails missing from hard-fought battles with cats. Alastair Parpington saw none of this — as soon as Mr Darkly had seen the door begin to open, he had mercilessly rugby-tackled the hotel inspector to the ground.

"What the *devil* do you think you're doing?" exclaimed Parpington through a mouthful of carpet.

"Erm…" Mr Darkly threw a pleading glance up at his wife, all the time frantic that the hotel inspector would soon hear the noise that dozens and dozens of rats cleaning plates and cutlery tends to bring. Not to mention the cursing, the fighting and the overuse of the word 'Arrrr'.

"It's… our… *carpet*, Mr Parpington," said Mrs Darkly, throwing herself underneath the table also, "isn't it… *clean*…?"

"I don't care how bally clean it is," the hotel inspector spluttered, "why did you throw me roughly to the ground?"

"Well..." Mr Darkly's mind began racing through the list of excuses for stupid things he had done. He usually only scrolled through this list when he was in trouble with Mrs Darkly. However, try as he might he just couldn't find an excuse good enough for rugby-tackling a hotel inspector underneath a dining-room table while dozens and dozens of rats that used to be pirates cleaned the plates and cutlery.

"He's *really* proud of our carpet," said Mrs Darkly.

"Here's an idea..." said Mr Darkly with a desperate, panicky glint in his eye. Mrs Darkly could tell that his brain was now having to work at approximately seven hundred times its usual speed. "Why don't we... crawl out of here — *WITHOUT LOOKING UP* — and admire the carpet as we go...?"

"Brilliant idea!" said Mrs Darkly before Parpington could speak. "Follow me, Mr Parpington!"

Grabbing his arm she began an awkward shuffling crawl over to the door, dragging a very bemused hotel inspector behind her. This bizarre ritual was accompanied by a running commentary on the state of their very clean, but ultimately not very conversation-worthy, carpet.

They were almost out of the room when, to their horror, they heard the kitchen door burst open and through it appeared Alphonse the zombie Maitre D'. He was carrying a particularly surly-looking Monsieur Volcan on his usual silver platter. Monsieur Volcan was busy overseeing that his dining room was being cleaned to his exacting standards when his eye fell on the decidedly unusual trio of crawling people making good their escape.

"What the *devil*..." he began. Mr Darkly, thinking quicker than he had ever done in his life, suddenly grabbed from the table beside him an uneaten and rather large crab-apple leftover from breakfast. With one almighty throw, he hurled it at the unsuspecting head. It struck Monsieur Volcan squarely on the forehead and sent him flying headlong (how else could he fly?) through the still swinging doors and back into his kitchen. Alphonse leapt after his boss, catching him just before he landed in that evening's beak and potato soup starter. There was a startled cry of "Sacre bleu!" as the kitchen doors swung shut.

"What was that?" Parpington's head shot up like a meerkat from its burrow. Thankfully, his beady little eyes saw only the swinging kitchen door before Mr Darkly rugby-tackled him once more on to the very clean, but ultimately not very conversation-worthy, carpet.

*   *   *

Meanwhile, upstairs Deirdre, Spectra and Uncle Dilbert were having a rather hard time convincing Millicent Parpington that hotel- room doors did indeed explode off their hinges quite a lot, actually. After the initial bouts of screaming (*mostly* from Millicent though Uncle Dilbert kept his end up heroically), Deirdre and Spectra eventually managed to calm them both down.

"You're so *horrid*, Eerie Deirdre. I knew your house would be horrid too!" Millicent was flapping around the room in a state, picking things up and moving them before putting them back down again in exactly the same spot. It was like she was a rather forgetful burglar. To be fair she had just been minding her own business when her door had exploded. That's enough to frighten anyone.

"Eerie Deirdre?" said Spectra, eyeing the small hippopotamus standing before her in a pink frilly bathing costume. "Why does she call you that?"

"I go to a *Typical* school, don't I?" Deirdre hissed. "We're all eerie to them."

"Speak for yourself," said Uncle Dilbert, as he casually belched a small puff of greeny-yellow smoke from his mouth while picking his nose and wiping a thick trail of glowing fluorescent snot down his overalls.

"I want you all to get out of here," sniffed Millicent. "Leave me alone. I'm going swimming."

Deirdre, Spectra and Uncle Dilbert all stepped clear of the now empty doorway (which was, I suppose, now there was no door in it just a... -*way*) and let Millicent through. It wasn't until Millicent had stomped down the hall and around the corner that Deirdre and Uncle Dilbert's eyes met.

"BARBARA!"

As one they both darted down the corridor and round the corner, leaving a very bewildered Spectra looking on. "Wait for me!" she shrieked as she ran after them. "Who's Barbara?"

Millicent was at the lift and had pressed the call button when Uncle Dilbert and Deirdre caught up with her.

"Don't take the lift!" they said at once.

Millicent looked at them suspiciously. "Why not?"

"It's broken!" said Uncle Dilbert. Which would have been fine if Deirdre hadn't shouted out, "Someone's been sick inside it!" at the same time.

Millicent's already high levels of suspicion cranked up another few notches. "So..." she eyed them both, "which is it then? *Broken or sick...* Because I'm sure Uncle Alastair would be extremely interested in a broken lift. Not to mention someone's sick that hasn't been cleaned up..."

Deirdre and her Uncle Dilbert stared straight ahead, each one wishing the other would speak. They both looked as though they were about to speak at the same time again when Spectra came gasping up behind them. "It's broken because of the sick," she panted. All three of them turned to look at her. "Before," she continued, "there was a... man... a... *big* man and he...threw up. Everywhere. In the lift, I mean—"

"It was nothing he ate *here*," Uncle Dilbert interrupted, "he ate somewhere else then came in... here... to... ride the lift..."

"Anyway!" Spectra snapped, giving Uncle Dilbert a withering look. "It all got inside the...mechanisms and now the lift won't work. But Deirdre's Uncle Dilbert is about to fix it, aren't you?" Spectra nudged Uncle Dilbert in the ribs, slightly harder than she would normally have done.

"*Oooff!* I mean — *yes.* I *was* just about to fix it. Won't take me a mo; why don't you three girls go out in the gardens? Lovely day for it..." This was stretching the truth a tiny bit, as there is no such thing

154

as a *lovely* day in Grimley-by-the-Sea. Any day without a thunderstorm or hurricane could be considered a lovely day.

"No!" Millicent stamped a chubby pink foot. "I want to go *swimming!*"

"Well then, let's go swimming!" said Deirdre, leading Millicent by the armband to the stairs. "Hurry up and fix that lift, Uncle Bert," she shot him a glare that told him to think of something to stop them all going down to the swimming pool very quickly. Poor Uncle Dilbert wasn't quick enough. Deirdre, Millicent and a considerably more befuddled Spectra soon found themselves tramping down the stairs and heading toward the basement.

Between their hearts pounding at every corner they turned and jumping at every shadow, the journey to the basement swimming pool seemed to take, instead of just a few minutes, approximately thirty-seven years. After making sure the changing rooms were well and truly empty, Deirdre ushered Millicent and Spectra inside before closing the door behind them and jamming a mop against it.

"Right," said Deirdre, "you get changed then, Millicent—"

"But I *am* changed," said Millicent, pulling the edges of her frilly, pink swimsuit.

"Of course you are," said Deirdre, looking helplessly at Spectra. "Then you just wait here and...do some...breathing exercises and we'll..."

"Go and take the cover off the pool...?" suggested Spectra.

"That's it!" said Deirdre, a little too enthusiastically.

She grabbed Spectra and raced through the changing rooms and into the pool area. She wedged the door shut behind them, this time with a large crate of inflatable rubber-rings.

Inside, the room was rather dark and dank. The only light came from the near wall, which was made up almost entirely of windows, and a small glass-domed skylight high up on the roof. Several new species of moss, fungi and plantlife had long ago made their homes along the heating pipes and in the damp corners. All of this was nothing, however, compared to the giant, purple, one-eyed octopus that was currently lolling in the pool itself, its stray tentacles flopping lazily out of the water on to the pool sides.

"What is *that*?" shrieked Spectra.

"Shhh!" Deirdre hissed back. "That's Barbara and we need to get her out of here!"

"Well obviously," said Spectra. "I sincerely doubt Little Miss Armbands out there won't notice... *Barbara*... But just exactly *how* are we supposed to get her out? She's the size of the entire pool!"

"Erm..." Deirdre looked about her.

"And if we *do* get her out," Spectra continued, most unhelpfully, "then where are we going to put her?"

Deirdre said nothing and looked around the pool once more as if the answer to their conundrum might just leap out at them. The room was quite bare, except for a few old chairs and sun-loungers (and, of course, the large swimming pool with the gigantic purple one-eyed octopus inside), but she doubted they could hide Barbara behind one of those.

"There's only one thing for it," said Deirdre.

"What?" said Spectra, knowing for certain that she wouldn't like the answer one little bit.

"We're going to have to *lure* her out."

"*Lure her out*?" said Spectra as though speaking to a very slow-witted hedgehog.

"To the garden," said Deirdre boldly, so that the insanity of her plan might be ignored. "There's a pond in the garden just big enough for her; all we need to do is get her into the conservatory —"

"The *conservatory*?" said Spectra as though the very slow-witted hedgehog was now a very deaf, slow-witted hedgehog.

"It's just through there," Deirdre pointed to the door farthest from them, "there's a great pair of glass doors that she'll slip through no problem and then it's just a short walk to the pond."

"Oh, sounds like a real breeze," said Spectra, with a familiar look on her face. "Meanwhile, how do we get her through *that* door?"

She gestured toward the door to the conservatory. It was just a normal-sized door, big enough to fit your average normal-sized Fright Folk through. An eight-limbed monocular monstrosity, however, was quite another thing. As if on cue the door burst open. The girls screamed in surprise as Uncle Dilbert ran in panting and sweating.

"S…sorry I'm l…late…" he bent double nursing a stitch. "Had to… had to run… round the other… side… SIDE!" He clutched his side as his stitch gave another ache, "… of the hotel…"

"Never mind that," said Deirdre unsympathetically,

"shut that door behind you, we need to get Barbara outside into the pond."

"You're having a laugh," said Uncle Dilbert, straightening up. "Get that thing outside? Are you mad?"

"No, but I may well be by the end of the day!" Deirdre snapped. "Instead of complaining, why don't you give us a hand? Make the doorway bigger, or make Barbara smaller, or…"

"Or make her disappear altogether!" said Spectra helpfully.

Uncle Dilbert and Deirdre looked at each other with uneasy expressions on their faces.

"Just do whatever you feel you can," said Deirdre, crossing all of her fingers behind her back.

"Well," said Uncle Dilbert, "here goes…" He waggled his wrists and flexed his eyebrows. Then he knotted his eyelashes and made his toenails glow bright purple before muttering some ancient enchantment and waggling all his stubby fingers in Barbara's direction.

The poor octopus knew something had gone terribly wrong before anyone else did. She began to rise slowly out of the pool, her tentacles floating serenely as though she was the first octopus in space. Deirdre and Spectra glanced briefly at each other, hardly daring to think that this half-baked plan might actually work. Barbara was almost touching the ceiling when slowly she began to swell. It wasn't very noticeable at first but soon she started to resemble an over-inflated balloon. Then she looked as though any moment she was about to *pop*, splattering the entire room in octopus spleen and ink. This made Deirdre start to panic.

"Uncle Bert!" she said tentatively. "Uncle Bert are you *sure* you know what you're doing?"

"Erm…" said Uncle Dilbert, his hands trembling slightly.

"Well, that's encouraging," said Spectra. "And look who's about to pay a visit…" She pointed toward the changing-room door and sure enough the handle had begun to rattle.

"Hurry!" shouted Deirdre, as the large crate of rubber-rings began to move.

Deirdre never quite knew how it happened (nor did Uncle Dilbert if truth be told), but instead of Barbara deflating, she swelled up even more. So much so that she soon resembled a novelty hot-air balloon. Deirdre and Spectra each grabbed a writhing tentacle and pulled with all their might. But now there was far too much hot air inside Barbara for the two of them to make any difference at all to her ever-increasing altitude.

"Help us!" Deirdre shrieked to Uncle Dilbert, who was still waving his stubby arms at the octopus. He stopped his flapping, ran over and grabbed a stray, flailing tentacle. The added might of the overweight wizard actually did start to make a slight difference and Barbara began very slowly to descend from the ceiling. Uncle Dilbert tugged and heaved with all his might in what had to be the most bizarre tug-of-war ever played and sure enough Barbara almost made it back down to earth again.

Almost…

With a sound like that of a thousand balloons all having the air forced out of them at once, the air inside

Barbara suddenly decided there was no place left to go. The octopus expelled the gas the only way she could, sending herself and poor Uncle Dilbert rocketing upward toward the glass skylight at perhaps two or maybe even *three* times the speed of sound.

Deirdre and Spectra had both (thankfully) let go of the Octopus One Way Express. They could do nothing but watch helplessly as Uncle Dilbert and Barbara flew boldly where no wizard, or octopus, has ever flown before. Straight up and out of the open skylight.

At that very moment Millicent forced her large frame through the changing-room doors, barging the crate of rubber-rings out of the way. She stood there panting, looking even more ridiculous now in her matching frilly pink swimming cap and goggles.

"What *is* going on in here?"

CHAPTER 14
THE MIDNIGHT MEETING

All in all the end of that first day couldn't come fast enough. Deirdre and Spectra had to stay with Millicent the entire time she was swimming to make sure that no-one unexpectedly walked in on her without Camouflage. Spending more than seven seconds in the company of Millicent Parpington was extremely hard work, so having to spend the entire day with her was akin to having your eyelashes pulled off by ravenous budgies. However, Millicent seemed absolutely *delighted* with her two new 'slaves' (as she thought them) and wasted no time in bossing them around at every available opportunity. It wasn't long before Spectra and Deirdre found themselves fetching Millicent exotic tropical fruit drinks and plates of chocolates, cakes and other treats whenever she snapped her fingers. There was a rather close call when Deirdre spotted that Spectra had brought Millicent a plate of freshly made strawberry sneezecake but had forgotten to scrape off the mucus.

It was almost midnight when the Parpingtons finally went to bed. Mr and Mrs Darkly had hired a carpenter to come and replace the door Uncle Dilbert had previously incinerated. Uncle Dilbert would normally have done it himself, but he had last been seen riding a highly-inflated one-eyed octopus out of a swimming-pool skylight, heading toward the horizon.

The Darklys, Spectra and Mortimer were all sitting in the lounge, none of them speaking and all of them tired beyond belief. Running around pretending to be completely Typical is a very tiring business indeed, especially having to wear Camouflage all day. Mortimer, who had no Camouflage, had kept himself locked up in his room the entire time and only now, after much coaxing from Deirdre, had he ventured downstairs for the meeting.

There suddenly came a sound from outside the lounge door. It was a kind of sloshing noise that made them all sit up at once, but it was only Uncle Dilbert. He also looked extremely tired, as well as incredibly wet, very bruised and beaten up.

"What happened to you?" asked Mrs Darkly, looking him up and down.

"Barbara," he replied gruffly as he dripped muddy water and pondweed all over the lounge carpet. "She did *not* want to go in that pond…"

"Bert," said Mr Darkly, "you're making a mess. We're being inspected, you know, can't you clean up after yourself?"

"Alright Dex," said Uncle Dilbert, "keep your fangs in." Uncle Dilbert wiggled his fingers and mumbled a few ancient magical words. Within a few minutes the carpet was on fire. He quickly put it out again, however, when he emptied the entire contents of both his boots and his bandana on to it. The wet lounge carpet was now a scorched, singed and even *wetter* lounge carpet. And it was decorated with several clumps of pondweed, a few confused halibut and one rather angry starfish.

"There," said Uncle Dilbert grumpily, "good as new. How long did you say this inspector was staying?"

"A week," said Deirdre miserably. "He'll be here on my birthday…"

"Aw, bad luck Deirdre," said Uncle Dilbert. "Tell you what, we'll have a big birthday bash right after he's gone, alright?"

"*If* we make it through this," said Spectra. The Darklys turned and looked at her.

"We?" said Deirdre with the tiniest hint of a half-smile.

"Well," said Spectra, trying her best to look her usual haughty self, "it's not just the hotel that'll suffer if we get found out. It's all of us, isn't it? And after today's fiasco I think you need me here."

"Too true," said Grandpa Horace, "the more hands on deck, the better. I remember when a busload of Japanese tourists arrived here by mistake sixty years ago. They were on their way to the Barkley Manor Hotel and Day Spa, but their bus driver had forgotten his reading glasses. Now *that* took some explaining I can tell you!"

"They were Chinese," said Grandma Hortense.

"Whatever, that's not the point," said Grandpa Horace. "The point is we've been through this before and we survived. We just have to use our brains, that's all."

Soon the lounge was bulging with hotel guests, crammed into every nook and cranny they could cram themselves into. Most of them still had their Camouflage on and, to the casual passer-by, may well have looked like an extremely *Typical* bunch. Except, that is, for those who had no Camouflage — like Bogby, or the trolls from Room 102, or Mortimer. They would

163

certainly raise a question or two, not to mention several eyebrows.

"Mortimer," said Deirdre, as she looked around the now very cluttered room, "is your Grandad coming to this meeting?" Mortimer was sitting next to her with a gently snoring Treacle on his lap.

"I don't know," he shrugged, stroking the snoozing tarantula, "probably not. He doesn't really like crowds and things."

Before Deirdre could reply there came the sound of someone tapping a glass with a knife. The general murmurings stopped as Mr Darkly stood atop the coffee table in the centre of the room, nervously straightened his red bowtie and dusted down his turquoise tank top.

"If I could just h-have y-your attention for j-just one m-moment…"

"Get on with it, Darkly!" said a rather bad-tempered mummy sitting in a corner wearing green striped pyjamas. The mummy was wearing striped pyjamas, not the corner.

"Let him talk," said an old ghoul waving an ear trumpet around, "and speak up, will you?"

"We are here," interrupted Mrs Darkly, "because there is a Typical amongst us." A general panicky murmuring started up again, and many accusatory glances shot around the room. "Two Typicals in actual fact," Mrs Darkly continued. "A hotel inspector and his niece have arrived unannounced and are planning on staying for the next six days. I know I don't need to tell you what will happen if they discover what we are."

"Well then," said an excitable bat hanging from

the chandelier, "we have to leave, don't we? We have to get out of here!"

"And go where?" came a voice from no-one, or rather an invisible someone. "We're here on holiday, where else can we go?"

"That's right," said a fat phantom on a chaise longue. "I'm quite comfortable where I am, thank you very much!"

"And what's more," said Mrs Darkly, "it won't look too good for us if all our guests leave unexpectedly, will it? We still have to pass the inspection."

"I hope he will not try and come into *my* kitchen," said Monsieur Volcan being held aloft, as usual, on his sliver platter by Alphonse the zombie Maitre D'.

"I think it's only a matter of time," said Mrs Darkly. "I hate it just as much as the rest of you, but, for the next few days we have to behave... *Typically*, I'm afraid. We'll just have to make a few changes, that's all."

"Like what?" shouted an angry werewolf woman with rollers in her fur.

"Well, for one, put on your ruddy Camouflage!" Uncle Dilbert bellowed across the room at her. The werewolf woman looked sheepish (as well as wolfish) then reverted to her Typical form. The rollers in her fur fell silently to the ground.

"Err... yes, thank you Dilbert," said Mrs Darkly. "And Graham...?" The huge ape was hanging upside down from the curtain rail by his feet eating a lemon-meringue pie, "I'm afraid you'll have to step down

165

from lift duty for the time being."

"Fair enough," he grunted.

"And Captain Blatch…?"

With a triumphant yell and a cry of, "Aye, me bucko!" Captain Blatch somersaulted from the back of a chair to the mantelpiece, swung by his tail from the chandelier and landed smartly on Mrs Darkly's shoulder.

"You and your crew will also have to make yourselves scarce, I'm afraid. I believe they're always on the lookout for cleaning crew at Grimley Academy: you and your men might try there for a summer job."

There was a cry of general ratty outrage as the rest of the Band of Brazen Buccaneers made their feelings known. However, they were soon quietened by their captain.

"It's alright, lads," he said, running along Mrs Darkly's outstretched arm and stopping in her open palm, "believe it or not, some Typical hotels don't appreciate our sort. Though most of 'em are infested with us." He leapt down on to the table and bowed low to Mrs Darkly, "Ye shall see neither tail-tip nor whisker of any of us, milady, ye have me word as a sea rat!"

"Thank you Captain," Mrs Darkly smiled. "Now, we just need to be careful and watch out for each other. If we all keep Camouflaged and don't do anything too… *un*Typical, then we might just make it out of this alright."

There was a bit more discussion and a lot more worry before everybody eventually trudged sleepily back to bed. Deirdre turned to Spectra and Mortimer and said, "What do you think of our chances then?"

166

"Fat and slim," yawned Treacle.

"Well one thing's for certain," said Spectra.

"What's that?" said Mortimer who still didn't *completely* trust Spectra even though she had, so far, proved co-operative.

"I'm going to need a place to sleep."

Deirdre and Mortimer looked at each other. "You're staying?" asked Deirdre in frank disbelief.

"Course I am," said Spectra haughtily, "you lot need *someone* around here who can get you out of trouble."

CHAPTER 15
DEIRDRE'S DREARY BIRTHDAY

The residents of The Darkly Manor Hotel, it has to be said, excelled themselves over the next few days. Despite the poor Fright Folk being on holiday, they tiptoed around every corner and kept their Camouflage up at all times. They also made sure their conversations were as dreadfully boring as possible and contained absolutely no mention whatsoever of the world immediately outside the hotel door.

There were a few near misses, however.

A few *very* near misses.

The next day, Mr Parpington decided he wanted to inspect the hotel from the very, very top to the very, very bottom. Mr Darkly was halfway toward the attic when he remembered that the pterodactyl who lived there might cause some concern for the hotel inspector. Just in time, Deirdre flew out of the hotel and around to the attic window to coax Kevin out that way before Parpington and Mr Darkly arrived. Kevin had been feeling distinctly neglected of late. As a result of all this excitement and of her punishment, Deirdre had not visited him in quite some time. So, he promptly refused to budge an inch and Deirdre was forced to drag him out by his claws. They had both just toppled out of the window when the attic door had opened.

The Darklys' cover was nearly blown a second time when Parpington bumped into Grandma Hortense one morning while she was out in the grounds jogging. Fortunately (for us all), Grandma Hortense tends to jog in the nude and, even more fortunately, she is, of course, invisible. Had she not been invisible, Parpington would have caught a glimpse of Grandma Hortense's blue bottom as he was extracting himself from a blueberry bush.

The hotel inspector also had the misfortune of meeting Grandpa Horace in the conservatory. Grandpa Horace was glaring intently out of the window at a small grey squirrel as Parpington walked in. He was eating a boiled cabbage and slug sandwich when, without putting it down or even turning his gaze from the conservatory window, said, "The squirrel's back."

Parpington looked from Grandpa Horace to the squirrel and back again. "Indeed?"

"Look at him!" Grandpa Horace continued. "Staring at me through the window, flashing me his tail, showing me his nuts—"

"I beg your pardon?" said Parpington, his ears reddening considerably.

"Look!" said Grandpa Horace, pointing at the squirrel who was indeed juggling three large brazil nuts.

Thankfully, Parpington was too busy staring at Grandpa Horace to notice. "Well..." he stammered, "can't you just...ignore him!"

"It's the *principle*," Grandpa Horace snapped back, "it's war!" Grandpa Horace stood up with remarkable agility for a Camouflaged werewolf his age, grabbed Parpington by the face, leaned in uncomfortably close and said, "I bought a giant bag of chocolate-covered brazil nuts, I ate all the chocolate off 'em, he *nicked* the bag and now he's burying them all over the garden! But not before parading them in front of me like a war hero! It's a good job I don't like brazil nuts…"

Parpington was unable to move. Whether it was because of the spry old man's grip on his face, or just utter confusion combined with abject fear, he was as still as a young Greek matador that had just lost a staring contest with Medusa. Medusa, for those of you who don't know, was a gorgon from Greece who could turn you to stone just by looking at you. This was quite a problem for Medusa as she (understandably) couldn't have any mirrors in her bathroom, or indeed in her entire house. As such she was, for a time, known locally as Medusa the Filthy Dirty Scruffbag. No-one ever said it to her face though.

"Erm…" the hotel inspector stammered, "p-perhaps you could b-buy another packet of chocolate-covered brazil nuts…? Let the squirrel have those?"

"I've *told* you!" Grandpa Horace and the hotel inspector's faces were so close together now that had someone walked in at that moment it would definitely have looked as though they were in the middle of a very passionate kiss. "It's the *principle* that matters," Grandpa Horace barked. "Today it's a packet of once chocolate-covered brazils, tomorrow it's the silverware and before you know it… *squirrels*! Everywhere! They've taken over the house!"

"I'm… *sorry*!" shrieked the hotel inspector, feeling more scared than he could ever remember being in his entire life.

"But I've got the solution…" Grandpa Horace pointed a gnarled finger out into the grounds. "You see that tree there?" Parpington followed Grandpa Horace's finger and saw a tall, green plant that looked a bit like a giant venus flytrap. "That's the Mongolian Squirrel-Snatcher…" Grandpa Horace paused for effect, but Mr Parpington was as affected as he was going to get. "I'm sorry it's come to this…" Grandpa Horace now had a crazed glint in his eye, "but I'm all out of suggestions…"

Parpington cleared his throat. "*Ahem*… P-perhaps you could just… buy a *bar* of chocolate if you don't like brazil nuts…?"

"It doesn't taste the same!" Grandpa Horace barked back. "They use different chocolate in chocolate *bars* than on chocolate *nuts* and I like chocolatey nuts!"

At that moment Mr Darkly burst through the door. He stopped for the briefest of moments as he tried to understand why on earth the hotel inspector and his father were locked in what appeared to be a very loving embrace in the conservatory. He was also mildly puzzled as to why they were being watched by a once-chocolate-covered-brazil-nut-juggling squirrel and a Mongolian Squirrel Snatcher. He realised mere seconds before it was too late what was about to happen. Mr Darkly grabbed Parpington rather too roughly by the wrist and dragged him (well, almost *threw* him) out of the conservatory just as the Mongolian Squirrel-Snatcher lunged on its unsuspecting prey. The squirrel never had a chance. The giant plant raised its ugly head in triumph and grinned. It bared two huge rows of knitting-needle-sized teeth, behind which the squirrel stood imprisoned.

Grandpa Horace gave a shriek of delight and danced a merry little jig. That is until, from nowhere, a long and very large purple tentacle slithered slowly into view. Without warning, it walloped the Mongolian Squirrel-Snatcher across the back of its head. The podgy plant spat out the now very bedraggled-looking and saliva-covered, but nonetheless incredibly grateful, squirrel. The fight that ensued between Barbara the one-eyed octopus and the Mongolian Squirrel-Snatcher was one that might well go down in history, but was only witnessed by one lone werewolf. A lone werewolf with a boundless affection for chocolatey nuts.

Meanwhile, Deirdre and Spectra were discovering that Millicent Parpington on her own (and without really trying) was more demanding than cleaning the entire hotel. Blindfolded. Whilst on fire. With both hands and feet tied together. On the rare occasions they were out of each other's sight, Deirdre and Spectra still had hundreds of jobs to do around the place. After all, they still had to pass an inspection and they didn't want to fail on account of something so comparably trivial as dirty toilets.

Deirdre's eleventh birthday eventually rolled around. To celebrate, she found herself with the glamorous job of floor-mopping. As if this wasn't treat enough, she soon moved on to scrubbing all the frames of the portraits in the main corridor. All the pictures' occupants had strange names and titles like: Lord Vladimir Darkly, Duke Cuthbert Fortescue Darkly XII, Doctor Caractacus Aloysius Darkly, Esq and (Deirdre's personal favourite) Field Marshall Hieronymous Babblington-Darkly. These were all Deirdre's ancestors and had lived in Darkly Manor before her family. As she scrubbed away with her scrubbing brush she wondered if any of them had ever spent their birthdays doing such a pointless task.

"If I ever have a portrait made," she said to herself, "I'll make sure it's known that no-one need *ever* scrub the frame no matter how filthy it gets. Especially if it's your *birthday*…"

Suddenly there came a noise from one end of the hall. It was a long hall and not very well lit so Deirdre couldn't quite make out what it was.

"Hello?" she said, her voice echoing down the hallway. "Spectra? Is that you?"

Suddenly, there came a terrific raspberry noise that nearly made Deirdre fall off her ladder. The raspberry was followed by the sight of a full suit of armour suddenly springing to life and charging headlong toward her, its arms and legs flailing wildly. Now things like this do occasionally happen in the Darkly Manor Hotel, but that doesn't mean that you get used to it. Deirdre shrieked and actually *did* fall off her ladder, only to drop her Camouflage halfway to the floor and glide gently the rest of the way. This did not, however, solve the problem of the rampaging suit of armour.

Slipping back into her Camouflaged state and grabbing her trusty mop, she leapt high into the air and charged the suit of armour head-on like a medieval joust of olde. Taking an enormous swipe like an angry lumberjack, Deirdre *whacked* the knight's head clean off, sending it spinning beautifully back up the hall. A marvellous spray of dark-green slime spewed out of it, covering the walls.

"My portrait frames!" Deirdre howled, as her once magnificently polished portrait frames now dripped green goo.

Cackles of laughter rang through the hall as the now headless knight suddenly removed his breastplate to reveal a glowing chubby green spectre that was giggling uncontrollably. It leapt out of the suit of armour and was quickly followed by another not-quite-so-chubby spectre that ran after it leaving bubbling, slimy footprints all over the just-mopped floor. In a rage, Deirdre picked up the mop bucket and hurled it after them. Unfortunately, this only served to cover the hallway floor with dirty mop water as well as bubbling green slime-footprints.

The infamous spectre twins from Room 304 splatted neatly through the door leaving one large and one not-quite-so-large blob of slime in their wake. Deirdre sighed and resigned herself to the task of clearing it up. She knew that the Parpingtons were out in the grounds playing tennis in the tennis courts. The moment they decided to move there was a rapid chain of reliable spies in place ready and waiting to relay the information back to the hotel before they got there.

"What's happened in *here*?" Spectra was walking toward her with a glass of something in each hand and a puzzled expression on her face. "I thought the whole point of this inspection was to pass it?"

"It was those two…" Deirdre searched longingly for a word to describe the spectre twins accurately, but no word in her vocabulary would suffice… "*spectres*," she eventually decided unimaginatively.

"Here," Spectra handed Deirdre a glass of crab-apple juice.

"Thanks," she took it and drank it almost in one.

"I'll give you a hand clearing up," said Spectra, "I'm finished washing the tablecloths and Wilhelmina's just drying them now."

They finished their crab-apple juices then headed for the kitchens to get an extra mop and bucket (not to mention refill the one Deirdre had thrown at the spectre twins).

"Having a happy birthday?" asked Spectra with half a smirk.

"Oh yeah, *brilliant*. Best ever. How did you know it was my birthday?"

"Heard your Uncle Dilbert talking about it this morning," said Spectra.

"Probably panicking because he's forgotten to buy me a present," said Deirdre.

"Yeah, that was it," Spectra smiled. She reached into her overall pocket and pulled something out. "Here," she handed it to Deirdre, blushing slightly.

Deirdre took it. "Thanks," she said, opening her hand to reveal a small bar of Freakish Delight that was slightly squashed and had melted a little bit. "Wow, thanks a lot. It's my favourite."

"I know," said Spectra, "I heard your family talking. I know it's not much, but..."

"It's great," said Deirdre, feeling quite as awkward as Spectra did. "Thanks. Here," she opened it and broke it in half, keeping one for herself and handing the other to Spectra.

"Oh," Spectra looked as though she had never

been offered anything in her life before now. She acted as if Deirdre had handed her not half a Freakish Delight bar, but half a stick of magical gold. "Thanks…"

They walked the rest of the way to the kitchens in silence, the only sound the quiet munching of two halves of a slightly squashed and a little bit melted bar of Freakish Delight. But though no words were spoken, that munching sound said and meant more than words probably ever could.

CHAPTER 16
NO BODY THERE

Deirdre and Spectra soon reached the kitchens and began refilling their mop buckets in the large sink. They were about to return to the main corridor to undo the work of the spectre twins (from Room 304) when it happened. The chain of events that would let them know when the Parpingtons were on the move went as follows:

1. At the first sign that the Parpingtons were about to finish their tennis match and head back to the hotel, the Mongolian Squirrel-Snatcher was to release a cloud of bright purple spores into the air.

2. Bogby Black (who would be hiding in a small clump of weeds in the garden pond) would see these spores and then signal with a crack of his whip-like amphibian tongue to Graham the great-ape, who was positioned on the roof of the hotel.

3. Graham would then bound across the rooftop and drop down to the door where he would signal First Mate Smothers of Captain Blatch's cutthroat crew. (First Mate Smothers, along with his captain, had bravely volunteered to stay behind at Darkly Manor while the rest of the crew vacated to Grimley Academy.) First Mate Smothers would then scurry across Reception to the dining-room door, which he would open before whistling three times like a cockatiel trapped in an ironing board.

4. Recognising the familiar sound of a cockatiel trapped in an ironing board, Captain Blatch would bang the dinner gong, thus signalling to the rest of the

hotel that the Parpingtons were heading back.

Simple.

Four simple steps to ensure safety.

Or so you would think.

This is what *should* have happened.

Here is what *did* happen:

1. When the Parpingtons finished their game of tennis, the Mongolian Squirrel-Snatcher, instead of watching and releasing a bright purple cloud of spores, was distracted by a rather cocky little grey squirrel. The squirrel was busy taunting an old man sitting in a conservatory by juggling what looked like several once-chocolate-covered brazil nuts. Thus the Mongolian Squirrel-Snatcher noticed far too late that the Parpingtons were on the move. In its panic, it released an over-large cloud of bright purple spores — that drifted over the garden pond and blinded poor old Bogby.

2. In his (quite literally) blind panic, Bogby bit his own tongue, which made it almost impossible to crack it like a whip and so signal Graham. Now panicking, and with a very swollen tongue, he attempted to explain his situation to Barbara the one-eyed octopus, who was also in the garden pond. Barbara had not been best pleased with her treatment of late. And who could blame her? Being ballooned up to gigantic proportions and then rocketed out of your home through the ceiling and then being forced to live outside in a pond is *certainly* no way to treat a lady. Even an enormous, eight-limbed, decidedly inky, one-eyed lady. As such, she was not paying a great deal of attention and so misinterpreted Bogby's mime for—

'crack-your-tentacles-like-a-whip-and-signal-Graham-who's-on-the-roof-that-the-Parpingtons-are-coming' — as — 'grab-me-about-the-waist-with-a-tentacle-and-hurl-me-toward-the-hotel-as-hard-as-you-possibly-can.

Now, speaking as someone who has seen both mimes, to give Barbara her due they are both quite similar. Unfortunately, we have neither the time nor the inclination to go into any in-depth analysis or comparison at this point. Let us just say that poor Bogby soon found himself hurtling through the air at a rather incredible rate of knots.

3. Unfortunately, once again, Graham was enjoying yet another slice of lemon-meringue pie (that ape *did* love his lemon-meringue pie) and was quite lost in its lemony, fluffy, egg-whitey goodness when he saw a small, amphibious blur come rocketing toward him. The small amphibious blur struck him in his rather large stomach (that's what too much lemon-meringue pie will do for you) and the two of them toppled off the hotel roof and landed in a heap on the ground below. Fortunately for Bogby, *he* landed on top of Graham rather than the other way around. Graham, on the other hand, didn't notice anything out of the ordinary. He continued eating his pie from the moment he fell from the roof, throughout the time he was falling toward the ground, and when he landed in a dusty heap on the ground.

4. Getting his breath, Bogby leapt to his feet and ran as fast as he could for the door. In his haste he swung the front door open a bit too enthusiastically and practically flattened poor First Mate Smothers between the door and the wall. The once three-dimensional rat

then staggered from between his door and wall sandwich and charged valiantly toward the dining room to alert his captain. Or rather *attempted* to charge valiantly toward the dining room to alert his captain. He got as far as a rather large crack in the wooden floor and, thanks to his now much-reduced mass, fell cleanly through it to the basement beneath. A faint splash could be heard as the poor rat fell headfirst into the (thankfully now octopus-free) swimming pool.

And so it was all down to Bogby. Bogby the Brave! Bogby the Bold! Bogby the Better-Get-a-Move-On-Cos-They'll-Be-Here-Any-Minute!

Graham had now finished his piece of lemon-meringue pie, got his concentration back and scrambled up the drainpipe and out of sight just as the Parpingtons rounded the corner. Bogby leapt for the dining-room door mere milliseconds before the Parpingtons crossed the hotel threshold. The door swung smoothly open and at the signal Captain Blatch (the only member of the warning chain to actually do his job correctly) banged the gong with all his ratty power.

Bogby hardly dared to breathe. He shuffled back to the wall and placed an ear against it, straining for any sound of movement. Deirdre and Spectra barged out of the kitchen, their faces masks of fear. On seeing Bogby breathless on the floor, both opened their mouths to ask questions. Bogby silenced them with an upheld webbed finger and the two girls joined him in holding their breath.

"Was that the dinner gong?" Millicent's awful voice carried through the silence like a burp in a church during prayer-time.

"Yes, Millicent dear," Mr Parpington's voice followed, "I do believe it was. I *am* rather hungry now that I think on, aren't you?"

"Oh *yes* Uncle," said Millicent, who was *always* hungry.

"Good. Then let's eat, shall we?"

Bogby, Deirdre, Spectra and Captain Blatch all froze. An unspoken panic rippled through them as they all realised the same thing at once.

The Parpingtons were coming...

Bogby leapt like a frog on fire into the kitchen just as Millicent and her Uncle Alastair entered the dining room. Captain Blatch and his Band of Brazen Buccaneers disappeared in that very magical way that all rodents can when faced with danger. This left Deirdre and Spectra standing there covered in a combination of dirty mop-water, spectral ectoplasm and portrait-frame polish.

"Ah," said Parpington, looking them up and down with ill-hidden disdain, "I take it dinner is about to be served?"

"Of course," said Deirdre, nudging Spectra hard in the ribs and thinking fast. "Here are some menus, and Spectra here will show you to your table..."

"Won't you step this way?" said Spectra with a smile as she slipped seamlessly into the hurriedly improvised plan Deirdre had set in motion. She sidled pleasantly alongside the Parpingtons with the intention of leading them to a table as far away from the kitchen as possible.

"I think *this* table will do nicely," said

Parpington, gesturing to a table for two immediately to his left. "Don't you agree, Millicent dear?"

"Oh *yes* Uncle Alastair," Millicent cooed, "I think this will do just fine."

"Certainly," said Spectra, pulling out each of their chairs. "Why don't I get you some drinks while Deirdre finds out what today's specials are? Deirdre?"

"Right," said Deirdre snapping back to reality, "yes, the specials. Won't be a minute!"

"Hang on there! I think I'll come with you," said Parpington, pushing out his chair and stepping forward. "I'd like a word with your chef: I haven't inspected the kitchens yet."

Deirdre felt as though the whole dining room was spinning. Their worst fears were being realised right in front of them. What's more, Alastair Parpington was heading right for the kitchen. The very kitchen wherein a disembodied head on a silver platter was most likely barking orders and being held up by a zombie Maitre D' named Alphonse. How do you explain *that* to a Typical hotel inspector?

"Wait!" Deirdre threw herself in front of the kitchen doors. "Our Head Chef... he, erm... doesn't like to be disturbed..."

"Well, young lady," Parpington puffed out his weedy little chest, "I have won the International League of Hotel Inspectors' Most Probing Person Award for nine years running. I did *not* win the International League of Hotel Inspectors' Most Probing Person Award for nine years running by *not* disturbing people. Now out of my way!"

Deirdre was running out of ideas. It was clear

that Parpington wasn't going to take no for an answer, but if he walked into the kitchen who knew what he might see in there? She was just about to rugby-tackle him to the ground (it had seemed to work for her parents) when all of a sudden something very strange happened. Monsieur Auguste Volcan's head peered around the kitchen door.

"Bonjour Monsieur Parpington," he said with a smile.

Deirdre was quite at a loss for what to say. Or *even* what to think. Unless Monsieur Volcan had somehow learned to hover in mid-air since this morning, or in his panic somehow grown a new body, *then* she might know what to think. But both (or either) of these possibilities were quite unlikely.

"Ah, Monsieur Volcan, I presume?" said Parpington, rocking back on his heels. "I trust you are ready for your inspection?"

"Alas," Monsieur Volcan replied, "I am not." At least, that's what he *said*. His tone was sad and filled with disappointment, his eyes downcast, and he definitely *said* he was *not*. Yet he was nodding. In fact, he was nodding long after he had finished talking. Nodding almost uncontrollably in fact, and no-one appeared to be more surprised than he at the vim and vigour with which he was nodding.

"I said *NON!*" he bellowed. The nodding stopped at once. "My apologies," he smiled his charming smile once more, "but we are in the middle of a minor catastrophe. Nothing that cannot be fixed, but I regret the kitchen must stay out of bounds for the near future."

"Nonsense," said Parpington taking a few more steps forward, "it can't be that bad, surely?"

"Yes, it is, quite, quite bad," Monsieur Volcan replied, though this time his head was shaking from side to side. Once again quite rapidly. "Although…" His head stopped dead.

"… it is…"

His head quivered slightly, as if it was unsure of what it might do next.

"… fixable…"

It nodded. Very slowly.

Monsieur Volcan broke into a large grin as though ecstatic that, for once in this conversation, his head had agreed with his voice.

"Do you think," Parpington continued, apparently eager to show why he had been the recipient of the International League of Hotel Inspectors' Most Probing Person Award nine years running, "that you might come out here to speak with me?"

"Non!" This time, head and voice matched up perfectly. In fact, Monsieur Volcan shook his head so vigorously that he appeared to slip halfway down the small crack he was peering through. This seemed to scare him as he gave a small shriek as he fell before muttering some words in French that Deirdre didn't think she wanted to hear in translation. "But I tell you what," suddenly a white-gloved hand had appeared around the door, "I shall cook you both a special treat for you are the hotel's special guests, oui?" The white-gloved hand formed an 'O' shape with its thumb and first finger, then moved toward Monsieur Volcan's lips, missed and instead flicked him in his right eye. "Sacre bleu!" bawled Monsieur Volcan as he disappeared around the kitchen door and it swung closed.

"I'll just see where your food is," said Deirdre, running through the kitchen door and slamming it shut behind her.

There, standing on an upturned mop-bucket, was Bogby, dressed in an overly large white chef's apron and carrying Monsieur Volcan's head in his white-gloved hands. "I did my best!" he squeaked.

"You did brilliantly, Bogby," said Deirdre, trying hard to suppress fits of laughter — which was very difficult considering she had just witnessed probably the most bizarre and ill-choreographed puppet show in the world.

"*Brilliantly?*" barked the Head Chef. "First your father throws an apple at my head and knocks me off my platter, then this *imbecile* nearly pokes my eye out with his flippers! I swear, if this place could cope without me I would resign!"

"Sorry, Monsieur Volcan," said Bogby.

"And another thing, you were nodding and shaking in all the wrong places!"

"Don't be too hard on him," said Deirdre. "He just got a little ahead of himself."

"Basic cleanliness," said Parpington as he dusted Barry, "is the cornerstone of *any* business. Especially the hotel business..."

CHAPTER 17
GRIM BUSINESS

All in all, between them they managed to make sure the Parpingtons' lunch went without any more hitches. Uncle and niece left, led back to their room by Spectra who simply *insisted* on showing them the way in case they got lost. As flimsy pretexts went, it wasn't quite as bad as Mr Darkly showing them the dining-room carpet 'up close', but it was still pretty bad.

That night, when the Parpingtons were asleep, Deirdre opened her birthday presents from her family. There was a new school bag from her parents and the copy of *A Frightologist's Field Guide* by Archibald Bott from her grandparents. Bogby's gift was the latest album from amphibious blues/rock trio The Green Street Freaks and there was also a jumbo bag of Gelatine Skeletons from Mortimer. Perhaps the most thoughtful, and definitely the most surprising, gift of all was the brand new compass from Uncle Dilbert.

"Went in that explorer shop you're always banging on about," he said with a smug look on his face, "Dr Deadstone's Danger Den. Asked them what you normally looked at when you came in. Do you like it?"

"I love it," said Deirdre truthfully. "Thanks Uncle Dilbert. Thanks everyone."

"Hardly the best birthday ever, is it?" said Mr Darkly, sympathetically.

"I don't mind," said Deirdre. "It's not like it's anyone's fault. Well, except Millicent Parpington's."

"Yeah," said Spectra, "when this is all over, I say

we send her a few Diarrhoea Dog-Biscuits in the post and see how she likes that. Has she got a dog?"

"Doesn't matter," said Deirdre, "she'd probably eat them herself anyway."

"Even better!" said Spectra, grinning.

"Well, as soon as the inspection is over," said Mrs Darkly, "how about we celebrate your birthday properly, Deirdre? How does a party sound?"

"Sounds great," Deirdre grinned.

Mr Darkly rubbed his eyes wearily. "I wonder if we'll even remember *how* to drop our Camouflage it's been so long."

"Ooh, don't even joke," said Mrs Darkly, "imagine having to live like those two. I couldn't look at myself in the mirror if I looked like *this*," Mrs Darkly gestured to her Typical face.

"I still think you look beautiful, Darcy," said Mr Darkly, leaning in and kissing her. Groans and wolf whistles (the latter from Grandpa Horace) erupted as Deirdre grabbed a cushion and buried her head in it. Parents could be so embarrassing sometimes.

"Well, goodnight all," said Grandma Hortense, yawning as she got up from her chair by the fire. "This time tomorrow it'll all be over."

And that time tomorrow, it most certainly was.

As it was his last day of inspection, Alastair Parpingon seemed intent on making the Darkly family sweat as much as possible before he left. He even conducted surprise room checks, completely at random. Poor old Little Willy Sprinkles leapt headfirst into the toilet as the hotel inspector burst through his door and shot through the U-bend at record speeds.

Not that anyone has ever measured the speed of a gremlin through a U-bend, but Little Willy was certainly on target for a personal best.

Parpington even began checking the bins to see if they were too full. Or too *empty*. All the while, he scribbled notes with his finely sharpened pencil into his little blue notebook, constantly making strange noises of derision by flaring his nostrils and rapidly blowing through them. It was most definitely all stations GO on that last day, and Alastair Parpington was going to make them well and truly work before he left.

Deirdre and Spectra soon found themselves scrubbing their scrubbing brushes so they sparkled like new. After that they were sent down to the library to see that all the books were in alphabetical order and that none of the pages were bent or creased in any way. After that, they headed to the dining room with a couple of rulers to make sure all the tablecloths were exactly the same distance off the floor.

Parpington had now begun interviewing staff individually and he cornered Wilhelmina while she was doing the laundry. Poor old Wilhelmina actually burst into tears at one point. She turned to run out of the basement, shrieking hysterically, before tripping over her own apron, somersaulting neatly and landing with a *splash* in a tin bath full of soaking delicates. She was so upset, it was all Mr Darkly could do to stop Mr Prendergast fetching his favourite rake and giving Parpington a jolly good thrashing.

Following her Uncle's example, Millicent Parpington had also become more unbearable than Deirdre had ever known. She had taken to carrying a small bell with her wherever she went and rang it almost constantly. Her idea was that Deirdre and Spectra were to come running the very second they heard the bell, but were to stay out of her sight whenever they weren't 'needed'.

"This has *got* to stop!" seethed Spectra after she and Deirdre had found themselves actually *carrying* Millicent upstairs to her room on the sixth floor. While she was being carried, Millicent had deigned to point out everything that was wrong in the hotel — from the direction it faced down to Mr Darkly's taste in bowties.

"Just a few more hours," Deirdre hissed to Spectra through gritted teeth. "Just a few more…"

It was the Camouflage that was the worst of it. Everyone in the hotel had been Camouflaged for a week and they were getting very bad tempered about it. It just wasn't natural for Fright Folk to be Camouflaged for so long. One dinnertime a scuffle had broken out between a vampire and a ghoul over half a bread roll. Young children kept forgetting what their parents looked like, because they had hardly ever seen them in Camouflage before. It was very hard to tell who was who in a hotel full of monsters that aren't allowed to be monsters, so when word spread that the Parpingtons were downstairs in Reception getting ready to check out, there was a veritable buzz of sheer delight that you could almost feel.

True to form, Parpington complained about *everything* in his final moments in the hotel. He claimed that the fountain pen he had been given to sign his bill with had too much ink in it, and that the mints in the bowl on the reception desk looked 'too randomly scattered'.

"I assume," he drawled, almost as if he wanted to drag out every syllable so as to take as much time as he possibly could, "that our stay here will be free of charge?"

Mr and Mrs Darkly both gritted their teeth and grinned back at him.

"Of *course*," said Mrs Darkly serenely, "it has truly been our pleasure having you here."

Parpington leant on the reception desk and looked around tapping the apparently over-filled fountain pen as his eyes meandered around the room. He didn't seem at all perturbed by the substantial crowd that had gathered to watch him leave. Indeed, he didn't seem to notice them at all. He was clearly looking for something, *anything* that might prolong his stay and therefore prolong the Darklys' agony.

"Good lord!" he pointed to the wall behind the reception desk. "That moose head is the dustiest thing I have *ever* seen!"

The next thing they knew, he was standing on a chair around the back of Reception with a feather duster in his hand, giving Barry the stuffed-zombie-moose head the dusting of a lifetime.

Now, as a rule it is rather impolite to dust someone when they are asleep. No matter how dusty they may be. The next time your granny falls asleep in front of the fire, it would be very rude indeed to go and get a can of polish and a cloth and give her a jolly good buffing. Just leave her alone while she dreams of rice pudding, brown bread and those boring butterscotchy sweets. Thankfully, Barry was usually a very heavy sleeper and only normally got dusted around once a year at Christmas time, when he would also have a large Santa hat on his head and baubles dangling from his antlers.

"Basic cleanliness," said Parpington as he dusted Barry, "is the cornerstone of *any* business. Especially the hotel business..." He was now buffing Barry with all the enthusiasm of an archaeologist unearthing a new type of dinosaur that breathed fire and spoke fluent Welsh.

The gathered crowd held their collective breaths (those that still *could* breathe) as the very observant of them saw Barry's nose most definitely give a slight twitch. Mercifully, Parpington was far too busy with his speech to notice something so trivial as a zombie-moose nostril flaring.

"There's no excuse for it," he continued, addressing the masses below him. "The paying public deserve a dust and dirt-free environment in which they can relax. Free from dust mites..."

Barry's nose twitched again.

"... free from rats..."

Barry sniffed in a rather large quantity of dust through his rather large left nostril.

"... free from cockroach infestation..."

Barry sniffed in a rather larger quantity of dust through his even larger *right* nostril.

"... free from grubs and earthworms and woodlice..."

Barry sniffed in the largest quantity of dust yet through his large left nostril *and* his even larger right nostril, culminating in an almighty —

"Aaaaa-choooo!!!"

Parpington stopped dusting and looked at the moose head. Barry's sneeze had — miraculously — not woken him up. It was a skill of his that he could do just about anything without waking up.

Eat.

Have a conversation.

Recite the lyrics to *Every Ghoul Needs a Guy*, the number one smash by one-hit wonders Marvyn Shufflebottom and His Orchestra of Ogres. Alastair Parpington, however, was left pondering the age-old question of whether stuffed moose heads can or cannot not sneeze.

"Right!" he leapt awkwardly down from his chair and ran back around the other side of the reception desk. "I have no choice but to tell you that this is, without question, the *strangest*, most *eerie*, most downright..." he seemed to be struggling to find the right word, "... *bizarre* hotel I have ever had the displeasure of staying in." He opened wide his arms and spun around, "I mean *look* at the place! It looks as though it hasn't been modernised since the Dark Ages! Dracula himself could live here and I bet even he'd find it a bit grim! There are noises in the walls at night. I feel like I'm being watched *all the time*! And I swear I saw a bat smoking a bubble-pipe earlier today..." Deirdre shuffled uncomfortably as Parpington marched over to the lounge. Most of the hotel guests with Camouflage had gathered there to see him go. "And your guests are," he continued gesticulating wildly at them, "without doubt, even stranger than the hotel!"

He rounded on Mr and Mrs Darkly, who were now holding hands tightly behind Reception waiting for the axe to fall.

"But," Parpington smoothed his too-slick hair and straightened his bowtie, "even I must concede that your facilities are... superb." A general gasp went around the room. "Your hotel is spotless," he shot a quick glance up at Barry who was still snoozing merrily away, before quickly looking back down again. "Your rooms are comfortable and your food... exquisite!"

There came a muffled cry of, "*Bon!*" from behind a very lumpy purple velvet cushion.

"I have no choice but to award you with the International League of Hotel Inspectors' Certificate of Approval." He pulled out a rolled-up piece of paper and slammed it on the reception desk. "Your hotel has passed my inspection... *just*." Disappointment was etched all over his face. "If I could deduct marks for... *weirdness* then you would surely fail miserably. But, as I cannot, then you must pass."

"Thank you," said Mrs Darkly through still-gritted teeth. She didn't trust herself to say anything more, nor even to open her teeth any wider.

"Thank you very much," said Mr Darkly, whose shaking knees were thankfully hidden by the reception desk.

Parpington looked at them in silence for several minutes more as though waiting for something to happen that might mean he could take his Certificate of Approval away. Alas, nothing did.

"Come on then, Millicent dear," he said, throwing his arms dramatically into the air and marching toward the door. "Let's go home!"

Mr Darkly grabbed their suitcases and led them

196

to the door. After checking (with his usual subtlety) that the coast was clear he escorted them outside. He returned several minutes later, slammed the door shut behind him and whispered—

"They've gone..."

There was an explosion of fur, fangs, claws, bandages and ectoplasm as everyone who was wearing their Camouflage dropped it and all those that didn't have it leapt, flew and burst from their hiding places. Monsieur Volcan was singing in a fine French tenor, while Alphonse swung the silver platter carrying him around in celebration. Uncle Dilbert was firing red, green, gold and purple sparks from his fat fingertips and no-one even minded the small fires that were erupting all over the place. Captain Blatch and his Band of Brazen Buccaneers had returned from their second job at Grimley Academy and were cart-wheeling, somersaulting and dancing merry pirate jigs. Field Marshall Wilberforce Pennington-Fothergill-Smythe was leading his Bat Battalion in some synchronised flying around the lounge and out through the open windows, barking orders and blowing bubbles as he went. Graham the giant gorilla had even put down his lemon-meringue pie and was dancing with Barbara and the Mongolian Squirrel Snatcher (who had long since put their differences aside) and a familiar-looking grey squirrel was showering the crowd with fresh, chocolate-free brazil nuts. Wilhelmina shrieked with delight and threw little Errol Darkly high up into the air as he whooped with laughter, and Mr Prendergast played a merry sea-shanty on the battered old violin he kept in his jacket pocket for just such an occasion.

Someone had let Kevin the pterodactyl out of the attic and he squawked and screeched merrily as he flapped around the ceiling like a giant bat. Everyone was hugging — even Spectra and Mortimer found themselves embracing as they danced around in a circle. The spectre twins were flinging slime at one another (and everyone else) but no-one seemed to mind because it was all finally over.

At least it *would* have been over if Alastair Parpington had not been standing in Reception at that very moment witnessing the entire spectacle after coming back for his forgotten notebook.

Awareness of his presence seemed to spread around the room quicker than gossip in a playground. Suddenly, somehow, everyone knew he was there □ and everyone froze. The seconds felt like hours as each and every monster, ghost, ghoul and pirate rodent in the room ran through a thousand possible excuses for how, why and what they were doing. No-one spoke for a very long time until there came a sniffling noise from behind Reception.

"Mmm," it said in a slow, sleepy voice. "I've been dusted… Is it Christmas already… Where are my baubles?"

This broke the silence perfectly.

Parpington leapt into the air in triumphal glee.

"I *KNEW* it!" he screamed, beating the air with his fists. "I *knew* you were all a load of freaks! Look at you all! How did I not see it sooner? It all makes so much sense now!" He was pacing up and down, his breathing getting heavier and heavier, sweat appearing in beads on his forehead. "I'll be famous," he lowered his voice and appeared to be speaking to himself. "I'll be world famous! Alastair Parpington, newly appointed Head of the International League of Hotel Inspectors. *Sir* Alastair Parpington, discoverer of... *freaks*! I'll tell the newspapers! I'll tell the newsreaders! I'll tell the WORLD!"

"*Ahem*," came a voice no-one recognised from behind him. "I'm terribly sorry and all, but I'm afraid that you... *won't*..."

From behind Alastair Parpington there stepped a tall, thin figure dressed very plainly in a long, black robe and a hood that covered the head and face entirely. In the stranger's skeletal hands were a long scythe and a rolled-up old piece of brown parchment.

"Who are you?" Parpington shrieked, clearly annoyed that his train of thought and plans for worldwide fame (and his own TV show) had been interrupted.

"My name is Reaper," said the stranger, "Mr G. Reaper, and I believe we have an appointment?"

"Appointment?" Parpington looked at Mr Reaper as though he were an idiot of the highest calibre. "I don't think so."

"Oh but I do, I'm afraid," said Mr Reaper, with all the politeness of a country vicar inviting the local knitting circle to tea. "You see, I've had this date written down here for ever such a long time," he unrolled the parchment and showed it to him, "and it's never wrong, I'm afraid."

Parpington peered in closer at the parchment. On it was written Alastair Parpington's name, the date, and underneath that, a time. Parpington wrinkled his face into a grimace and straightened up again. "What is this nonsense?" He looked around the room but no-one said anything. "Who wrote this?" He turned back to the piece of old parchment. "Which one of you knew my middle name was Miriam? Eh?" Still no-one spoke. "Well, you've got the date right at least, but the time's wrong," he looked at his watch, "according to *my* watch there are still twenty seconds to go until…"

He tailed off. Slowly, but very surely, the cogs in Alastair Parpington's brain were beginning to turn. "Mr G. Reaper…" he muttered to himself. "App… appointment…"

Twenty seconds later, Alastair Parpington stiffened where he stood, his eyes widened and he dropped stone cold dead.

"Right," said Mr Reaper, "sorry about all that." He handed a pen and the roll of parchment to Mrs Darkly before turning to the other Fright Folk who stood agog. "And sorry to all of you that I haven't introduced myself earlier. I just like to get the business over with first — I'm sure you understand. An awful lot of stigma attached to this job, you know. Could you just sign and date at the bottom please? That's great, thanks." Mrs Darkly handed the parchment and pen back. The whole of the hotel was in silence. Mr Reaper rolled the parchment back up and placed it inside his robe along with the pen.

"Oh," he said, noticing a familiar face in the crowd, "hello Mortimer. Alright?"

Mortimer waved at his grandfather before turning to Deirdre. "He did say he was here on business…"

EPILOGUE

(Which means the end-y bit, you know, after the actual story.)

Deirdre, Spectra, Bogby, Mortimer and Treacle sat in the lounge amidst the wreckage of what could honestly be called one of the best birthday parties in Grimley history. All five of them had eaten far too much, danced far too much and were now feeling very full, very tired and more than a little bit sick.

"I can't believe your grandad killed the hotel inspector," said Spectra for perhaps the thousandth time.

"He didn't *kill* him," said Mortimer for what felt like the thousand and first time. "He doesn't *kill* anyone; that was just Parpington's time, that's all. You saw that piece of paper, everyone's got one."

"Alright, keep your skull on," Spectra smiled. "I was only joking."

"It would have been nice if someone had changed that date to one week *earlier*," said Deirdre.

The others murmured their agreement.

The events of the day had, understandably, been all anyone could talk about. It had been Mr Darkly who had gone out to the car to break the news to Millicent. Millicent had taken the news remarkably well, replying — "Oh well, he never really gave me very good Christmas or birthday presents anyway."

After a suitable period of mourning (around seven to ten seconds) the celebrations had started, lasted almost the entire day and had only just finished. The culmination of relief, joy and the fact that no-one had to wear their Camouflage anymore resulted in a party that The Darkly Manor Hotel would not soon forget.

"Well," said Spectra getting to her feet and yawning, "I'd better be going home."

"Me too," said Bogby.

"I'll walk with you if you like," said Spectra. The others all turned to look at Spectra, who looked bewilderedly back at them. "What?"

"Spectra Ghastly," said Deirdre, "I think you might be in very imminent danger of becoming an almost decent monster."

The others laughed, even Spectra. "Maybe," she smiled, "just don't go spreading it around, alright?"

They walked over to the door and looked out over the village. In the moonlight they could just make out the silhouette of Grimley Academy high on a hill on the far side of Grimley-by-the-Sea.

"We'll be there in a couple of weeks," said Bogby. "Grimley Academy."

Deirdre and Spectra murmured and nodded. "What about you, Mortimer?" asked Deirdre. "What school are you off to?"

"Well..." said Mortimer, "I've been writing back and forth to Mum and Dad over the holidays and, well, there aren't that many good schools in The Underworld, not as good as Grimley Academy anyway. Plus my grandad's got a house in Grimley, a kind of holiday home for when he's not working. So, it looks like I might be sticking around."

"Brilliant!" said Bogby, punching Mortimer on his bony shoulder.

"Why didn't you tell us?" said Spectra.

"Well," Mortimer shrugged, "you seemed so… *busy* all summer, I didn't really get the chance."

"Too right," said Deirdre, whose joints still ached from all the scrubbing, mopping and endless polishing. "If I never see another scrubbing brush, mop, bucket of water or can of polish again I'll die a happy gargoyle. But don't tell your grandad, Mortimer."

They laughed as the moon came out from behind a cloud and lit up the village before them.

"What do you think it'll be like?" said Spectra. "School, I mean?"

"Oh, you know school," said Deirdre, "how much fun could it be…?"

About the Author

Adam Perrott has no middle name and so will, on occasion, invent one for comedic purposes. His two favourites are Benedict and Shakespeare (in that order). He has been a struggling actor, musician, singer/songwriter, comedian of sorts and writer and hopes to remove the word 'struggling' from this list of past occupations in the not-to-distant future. He lives and writes in a room full of books that he has collected and brought together to inspire him. His time is used up, in the main, by his two-year-old son Caleb who enjoys throwing. His editor awoke him this morning to write this. His revenge will be swift...